TWICE A KISS

TWICE A KISS

TWICE A KISS

Carol Wood

CHIVERS

British Library Cataloguing in Publication Data available

This Large Print edition published by AudioGO Ltd, Bath, 2013.
Published by arrangement with the Author.

U.K. Hardcover   ISBN   978 1 4713 2386 7
U.K. Softcover   ISBN   978 1 4713 2387 4

Printed and bound in Great Britain by
MPG Books Group Limited

CHAPTER ONE

The train was late. Erin checked the time again and found to her irritation that both the station clock and her watch were agreed at ten minutes past eleven—twenty-five minutes past the arrival time of the train from London.

Two announcements over the loudspeaker and one cup of coffee later, Erin finally heard the distant thunder of wheels. A slight fluttering near her heart coincided with the rush and swoosh of the carriages as the train drew slowly to a halt.

There were only a handful of passengers who alighted at Hayford Minster station, a small rural market town in the heart of Dorset. Glancing at each face in turn, Erin wondered if the man she was about to meet would recognise her. The last time she had seen Nick, her long, dark brown hair had touched her shoulders—long enough to sweep into the chignon style she had decided to wear under her wedding veil . . .

Automatically Erin drew her thoughts back from the summer of the previous year. Then it had seemed she had everything to look forward to—marriage to City stockbroker Simon Forester at the picturesque Minster, a honeymoon in the beautiful cottage they had bought and a rural lifestyle of which she had

1

always dreamed.

But all her dreams had been shattered when Simon had failed to turn up on their wedding day. It had been a long and slow recovery since then and now Nick Hanson was arriving back in England, stirring up memories she would prefer to forget, causing unwanted recollections to surface inside her.

Erin took a deep breath. She had no intention of allowing Nick's presence to upset her. She *could* handle this. She *had* come to terms with what had happened last summer and had moved on with her life.

Anyway, by all accounts Nick had fared little better, Erin reminded herself as she glanced quickly at each figure walking along the platform. His stormy relationship with the Canadian television newscaster Sherry Tate had resulted in his decision to return to England—a fact which he probably did not want to elaborate on, any more than she did her broken engagement to Simon.

Erin lifted one slender—and ringless—hand to push back the wing of hair that gently shielded her lovely emerald eyes. She had every intention of making Nick welcome—driving him to the mews, providing him with the keys to the flat—then saying a polite but firm goodbye until Monday when, at the surgery, they would meet on an entirely professional footing.

'Erin?'

The voice startled her, propelling her back in time and causing the fine hairs on the back of her neck to stand on end. She turned and met the brown eyes of the man she had been awaiting, eyes that were assessing her shrewdly.

'Nick!' she gasped. 'Where did you spring from? I . . . I didn't see you get off the train.'

The tall, dark-haired man leaned forward and she stiffened, turning very slightly as his lips brushed her cheek. For a moment he looked puzzled. 'That's because I wasn't on it,' he said, straightening up.

Erin's gaze went over the broad shoulders hidden beneath a casual white T-shirt, the vest tucked into the waistband of a pair of light blue jeans that skimmed over slim hips and hugged long, muscular legs. There was something different about him, she realised as they stood there, each taking in the physical changes that had occurred over the last thirteen months. At thirty-three years of age Nick was as fit and athletic-looking as ever, but there was a look about him that was more brooding than before, the expression that filled his gaze wary.

'You weren't on the train?' Erin tried to keep both the surprise and confusion from her voice.

'Too many delays in the City,' he explained easily, 'so I hired a car at Heathrow and drove straight down. I rang you earlier this morning

3

and had no reply. Finally I phoned the surgery and told them what I was doing. I did hope they might get a message through to you.'

'No,' she answered hesitantly. 'I left my pager at home since I wasn't on call.' She had taken a jog, had a shower and after a swift breakfast she had made a shopping trip to the market for fresh vegetables and fruit. Fully expecting to meet Nick from the train, she hadn't hurried.

She looked up, her eyes meeting his, and they stood for a few seconds in awkward silence, then both spoke at once, their voices drowned as the train began to pull out of the station.

'Let's get out of here, shall we?' he said eventually, and, taking her arm, he led the way to the gate. Together they walked through it and out into the bright sunshine of the July morning. Parked on the far side of the car park was her blue hatchback and beside it was a dark red Ford to which he gestured. 'I've leased it for the month while I look around for something to drive,' he told her as they walked by the taxi waiting area and towards the cars. 'I went to the surgery first, but it was closed.'

Erin nodded. 'We hold an eight-thirty to eleven surgery on Saturday mornings and the girls close fairly sharply afterwards.'

They had stopped by the Ford and Nick smiled down at her. 'It's good to see you again, Erin, really good.'

She met his gaze, recalling the intense deep brown lustre of his eyes and that certain way he had of looking at her, the way that Simon had never looked at her . . .

Clearing her throat, she said quickly, 'Well, I'm sure you'd like to get settled and freshen up. I'll take you to the flat and show you around.'

He nodded, a flicker of puzzlement in his eyes. 'Yes, thanks, I'd like that.'

She was aware that her attitude was creating a distance between them and that was what she intended. Although she had no wish to seem unfriendly, she wanted to make it clear that she had no intention of alluding to the past.

The fact that Nick was renting the flat beneath hers would make little difference to her. It was for Alissa's and Max's sake that she had agreed to act as a negotiator with the agency. Alissa and Max Darvill, the senior partners of Minster Practice, had suggested that the vacant ground-floor flat would be just the place for Nick to rent on his return to England. Close to the surgery and located in a beautiful area by the ancient Minster, it had seemed the perfect choice. As Nick Hanson was a relative of Alissa's, and had been a locum for a short time at Minster Practice the previous summer, Erin had felt obliged to help.

'I'll follow you,' Nick called as she unlocked

her car. She gave him a brief nod and climbed in, relieved that at last this part of the day was over.

The journey from the station to her home by the Minster took less than a quarter of an hour, and when she turned her car into the cobbled lane and parked outside the mews the dark red hired car pulled in just behind her. Erin glanced in her driving mirror and saw Nick climb out. He stood there, looking up at the elegant red brick building with its pretty window-boxes spilling with summer flowers.

For a moment her heart raced and she sat very still, her eyes lingering on the tall, athletic figure that stared up at her first-floor flat. As she watched him, she recalled the time they spent together last year . . . a trip to the New Forest and then a leisurely drive back to her flat to sit drinking coffee as they'd sat on the balcony. That night, as they'd said goodbye, she had looked up into those dark brown eyes and had known that she hadn't wanted the evening to end.

Erin shook her head a little as if to dislodge the memory, then climbed out of her car. Taking her keys from her handbag, she opened the second of the two doors and walked in. The flat was surprisingly large, its rooms smelling slightly musty. The previous tenant had vacated six months ago and it had been vacant ever since.

Nick stood on the bare-boarded floor of the

downstairs room and gazed out of the window onto the garden. 'It's charming,' he said quietly. 'I appreciate your help in arranging it all for me.'

'No problem.' Erin shrugged casually. 'My landlord's happy for you to take on a short lease, but after Christmas my flat will become vacant . . . so if you want the option of moving upstairs I'm sure it can be arranged.'

He turned to face her, looking at her with an intensity she remembered so vividly. His eyes held hers as one eyebrow arched. 'So you've made up your mind to leave Hayford Minster after all?'

She nodded. 'Yes . . . yes, I have.'

'And has your decision anything to do Simon Forester?' he asked, his gaze seeming to probe deeply into her mind as she hesitated then quickly pulled herself together.

'I told you on the phone, Nick—' she began, but he cut her short.

'I couldn't see your face on the phone, I could only hear what you wanted me to hear,' he interrupted, and suddenly the atmosphere in the room seemed to change, an electric charge running between them as they stared at one another. 'I couldn't read the expression in your eyes,' he went on, his gaze not leaving her face. 'Did Simon hurt you enough to make you run away and leave all that you've worked so hard to achieve?'

The question shocked her. She didn't want

to discuss Simon with anyone, least of all Nick. She had no intention of being subjected to an inquisition over her feelings towards her ex-fiancé and, lifting her chin, she said dismissively, 'Since you ask, as far as Simon is concerned, that part of my life is over and in the past. There's no reason for me to run away, even though you seem to have made your mind up that that's what I'm doing.'

Nick left the window and walked towards her, his eyes narrowed as he advanced on her. 'Is that the truth, Erin?' His voice was low, challenging, and a dart of fear went through her. 'It's my guess that you haven't come to terms with happened last summer and that, rather than face acknowledging your feelings, you'd prefer to run from them. Tell me if I'm wrong, Erin. Look me in the eye and tell me.'

For a moment she couldn't reply, her throat dry as she swallowed in an effort to speak. When she found her voice it seemed unnatural even to her own ears. 'You're wrong,' she said abruptly, avoiding his laser-like stare. 'Now, I really must be going.'

His eyes flickered and for a moment she thought he was going to speak, his lips twitching as he gazed at her, the atmosphere around them tense. Then she recovered herself and delved into her handbag. 'Here are the keys to your flat—the Yale for the front door, the other for the back.' She handed them to him, dropping them into his hand—a hand that moved up reluctantly to accept them. 'I've stocked your fridge with a few groceries, enough for the weekend, anyway. If there's anything else you need—'

'Erin!' He stepped forward, effectively blocking her way. 'I need to talk to you. *We* need to talk. Are you free this evening?'

'I'm afraid I've made arrangements for tonight,' Erin said evasively as she glanced toward the door. 'Goodbye, Nick.'

In one swift movement she stepped to the side, unlatched the door and closed it behind her. With trembling fingers she searched for her own key and hurriedly inserted it into the lock of the adjacent door.

Once inside her own flat, she stood still, staring at the flight of stairs before her. Then, allowing the breath to flow from her lungs, she closed her eyes and sank back against the cold wood of the door. Why did he disturb her in this way? Why had she taken such a defensive attitude with him? What was she frightened of?

For a few seconds she waited for her heart to stop racing. When it had finally slowed to a reasonable rate she swallowed, opened her eyes and began to ascend the stairs.

An instinct deep inside her told her that whatever it took to maintain her distance from the man in the flat below, she must. For reasons she wasn't entirely sure of, his presence had upset her more than she had bargained for. And, if she was truthful, she couldn't put it all down to the link with Simon. Nick Hanson *was* a reminder of the past. But there was something else, something she didn't understand—or was it that she didn't want to understand?

As for what he had accused her of—running away—that was ridiculous. She was simply taking a new direction. And it was a point of view she had no intention of defending—to anyone, including Nick Hanson.

*   *   *

Dr Alissa Darvill looked from the window and then back to the carry-cot in which baby Jake slept. Alissa was sitting in her husband's consulting room as Max escorted out his last patient. She waited for him to return, listening to the sound of her brother-in-law's voice in the corridor as he, too, said goodbye to his patient.

Nick, her brother-in-law from her first marriage, had decided to return to England from Vancouver to take the place of Alec Rogers, the retiring partner. Nick's relationship with Sherry Tate, the Canadian newscaster, was now over. Alissa hoped that, despite their break-up, he would settle well to the practice and life in Hayford Minster.

Alissa thoughtfully brushed back a lock of fair hair. Last summer she'd been sure that

Nick and Erin, her twenty-nine-year-old junior partner, had been attracted to one another. But Erin had been engaged at the time, though her marriage had since been called off . . .

Alissa sighed deeply at this thought, looking distracted as her husband walked in. He closed the door behind him and, walking across the room, bent forward and kissed her forehead. He raised his eyebrows at the sleeping infant.

'Next feed?' he whispered. Their hands linked, they stared down at their beautiful baby son.

Alissa laughed softly. 'Any moment now, I expect.'

Max nodded, taking his wife into his arms. 'Have I told you lately how much I love you?' He tipped her chin up and kissed her lightly. 'Because I'm about to tell you again.'

Alissa breathed in his scent, recalling the events that had brought them to this day, almost unable to believe how happy she was after eight months of marriage.

Priss, Max's troublesome first wife, was now living in Paris with her new husband and baby daughter. Max's two sons and Alissa's young daughter and baby Jake made up their family of six, Alissa's own unhappy first marriage long forgotten as she recalled the joy with which baby Jake had entered the world. Her heart went out to Erin who deserved so much more than the heartless Simon Forester.

'What's that frown for, Mrs Darvill?' Max

11

murmured as Jake stirred.

'I was thinking of Erin,' Alissa murmured reflectively. 'Has Nick mentioned anything to you?'

'About what?'

Alissa glanced at her husband. 'I thought he might have said whether or not he likes the flat.'

Max shrugged. 'As far as I know he does. Why?'

'I was wondering,' Alissa suggested hesitantly, 'if Erin and Nick would care to be godparents to Jake?'

Max sat down at his desk, leaned back in his chair and studied his wife with an amused expression. 'Do I detect a hint of matchmaking here?'

Alissa paused, her blue eyes innocent as she turned and smiled softly. 'Not at all.' She waited as Max grinned again, his grey eyes sparkling under his shock of black hair. 'But, as you happen to mention it, I did think they got on rather well last year, didn't you?'

Max was thoughtful for a moment. 'Last year perhaps. But, since then, don't you think the situation has changed rather?'

Alissa lifted baby Jake into her arms and rocked him.

She looked up at her husband and raised her blonde eyebrows. 'Yes, I suppose you're right.'

Max looked at his wife, then, slowly leaning

12

forward, he rested his elbows on the desk. 'Darling, I give you full marks for trying. Just remember, though, a lot of water has gone under the bridge since last they met. After Sherry, Nick is no rush to become involved and Erin is, she says, determined to leave general practice for private practice in London.'

Alissa nodded distractedly. 'Yes, that's true, but I have a feeling—'

'And I have a feeling,' commented Max ruefully as baby Jake opened his blue eyes and gurgled, 'that our son is hungry.'

Alissa stroked her finger across the tiny pink forehead and the wisp of jet black hair, experiencing a wave of deep pleasure as she gazed first at her son and then at her husband. Whatever Max said—and she knew he was right—she was still resolved to ask Erin and Nick to be godparents to Jake.

*　　　*　　　*

Erin's last patient of the Friday babies and toddlers clinic, a two-and-a-half-year-old toddler, sat on his mother's lap, looking at Erin with wide blue eyes. Esme Kelly, his mother, pulled on his nappy and vest and smoothed her hand over the curly mop of black hair.

Erin reached out and little Orion grasped her finger, eager to test it between his teeth. She removed the temptation, dropping her hand to his toes and giving them a wiggle.

'So you think he's all right, Dr Brooks?' Esme asked again. 'This is nothing to do with his operation or anything like that?'

Erin shook her head and smiled. 'No, Orion's testis is perfectly normal, there's no sign of any problem, Esme. The reason he isn't responding to toilet training is because boys are generally later than girls in developing bowel and bladder control. At this stage his immature bladder can't hold urine for very long. He can't wait for you to produce the potty so accidents happen.'

'But I try to teach him to sit on the potty.' Esme sighed. 'It's always available. He just can't seem to reach it in time.'

Erin nodded. 'Yes, it's an awkward phase. But little boys can only hold onto urine for a minute or two. Why don't you try trainer pants during the day?'

Esme paused. 'I suppose so. I was just hoping that he would begin to stay dry during the day even if at night he had accidents. I've tried so hard with him.'

'Is Orion still at a crèche?' Erin asked.

Esme nodded. 'I work in the mornings at the library. It helps towards the rent. Sky can't always send money. At least, I can't rely on it.'

'Does Sky visit you?' Erin asked.

'When he can. But travellers are always on the move.' She looked at Erin with her son's large, sad blue eyes. 'He's involved with

14

someone else now, anyway. He wrote saying that although he'll try to send what he can he's got a baby on the way.'

Erin felt a pang of sympathy for twenty-year-old Esme Kelly, formerly known as India. After leaving school, Esme had joined the travellers against the wishes of her parents. The group had come to stay in Hayford Minster last year. Her partner, known as Sky, had objected to little Orion's operation for an undescended testis, believing that surgery was not necessary.

The child had been at risk and it had been Esme who had consented to the operation, which was successful and the child restored to good health. But by then Esme and Sky had separated and Esme had decided that her future did not lie with the travellers, choosing to remain in Hayford Minster when the travellers had moved on.

'How is Dr Leigh and her baby?' Esme asked suddenly. 'Wasn't it a premature birth?'

Esme had been Alissa's patient before Alissa's marriage to Max and had then transferred to Erin during Alissa's pregnancy leave from the surgery. 'Mother and baby are doing well,' Erin assured her. 'Jake was a month premature, but he's up to weight now and a bouncing little boy.'

'I met Dr Leigh and her daughter and stepson in the supermarket just after Christmas.' Esme smiled. 'They seemed so happy. I'm really pleased for her. She was very kind to Orion and I when Sky left us. Will she be coming back to the surgery?'

Erin nodded. 'Yes, as soon as she feels confident to leave Jake, she'll be with us part time.'

The young woman nodded, her dark hair tied back in a ponytail, as opposed to the dreadlocks she'd previously worn, and her long skirts and thongs had now been swapped for jeans and a casual shirt. In the year that she had been a single mother she had tried hard to find roots for her little boy and herself. It wasn't easy, Erin knew, as she was estranged from her parents and now, it seemed, from Sky.

'Returning to Orion,' Erin continued as Esme lowered the boy into his pushchair, 'let me reassure you that Orion is physically well. The toilet training will be successful in time. Just allow him to find his own pace without any pressure. Don't make a drama out of it, but be pleased when he does perform. Relax and I think you'll find he will relax with you.'

'OK, Dr Brooks, I'll try. See you at the next clinic.'

Esme guided the pushchair to the door and out into the hallway, looking up at someone who was approaching and saying hello. The deep voice that replied sent a faint tremor through Erin as the door opened and Nick stood there.

'Hi, there,' he said uncertainly. 'Are you free? May I come in?'

Erin nodded. 'Yes, of course.'

He walked in, his tall figure clad in a pale blue polo shirt and dark chinos. His dark brown hair had grown in the two weeks he had been in Britain, and he casually thrust it back over his head with tanned fingers as he sat down in the chair by her desk.

He smiled as he looked at her, a smile that touched his brown eyes under their thick black lashes. 'That was a striking child,' he said.

'Yes,' Erin agreed. 'Orion Kelly.'

'Orion? As in the stars?'

'As a matter of fact, it is. His mother was once called India and his father, a traveller, is called Sky.' She explained in brief the family's history.

'It's hard to imagine that a man could bear to be parted from a family like that,' he said quietly. 'Is there no hope of a reconciliation?'

Erin shook her head. 'I don't think so. He's found someone else, apparently, and there's a baby on the way.'

'I saw a patient this afternoon who's had a similar experience.' Nick frowned as he leaned back, one muscular arm thrown over the back of the chair as he paused. 'He's attempting to save his marriage—not very successfully, I regret to say. They have one child, a little girl called Marina. She came to the allergy clinic with her father and saw Mo, the nurse. Mo asked me to see her and so I did. The rash began this year, when the mother left. The father is worried that all the trouble is taking its toll on the six-year-old.'

'What is the current situation?'

'Marina has a severe rash on her neck and chest. Her mother is living with another partner. The child goes to see her at weekends. That's when the rash seems worse.'

Erin frowned. 'And you believe it's connected?'

He shrugged. 'I don't know, but Pauline Ford has been your patient for the last two years, according to her husband, Desmond.' Nick lifted his dark eyes. 'Is there any chance of you speaking to her, do you think?'

'Pauline Ford?' Erin turned to her keyboard and tapped in the name. She waited for the screen to flash up the details, then looked back at Nick. 'I've seen Pauline Ford twice only. What had you in mind?'

Nick looked at her, then said, 'Could you ring her or write to her in connection with Marina?'

Erin hesitated. 'Has Desmond Ford suggested this?'

'No. It was my idea.'

'Nick, I—'

'You don't want to do it?'

Erin gestured to the screen. 'As I said, I've seen Pauline Ford only twice. I know very little of her history. And I don't know her husband

18

or daughter at all. Have the Fords tried counselling?'

'They have, but to no avail.'

'If professional counsellors have failed to help, Nick, I don't see how we can. In fact, it might seem like we're interfering.'

'So it's no?' Nick looked at her levelly.

Erin sat back in her chair with a sigh. 'I'm not sure, Nick. I'll think about it.'

For a moment they were both silent then he sat forward, his elbows resting on his knees. He glanced up at her, one dark eyebrow crooked. 'Erin, this is probably neither the time nor place, but I think it's important we talk. And I'm not referring to the Fords. We need to talk about last year and about what happened to us.'

Erin looked down at her hands. 'There's no point in—'

'I think you're frightened, Erin.' His voice was low as he interrupted her. 'Of what, I don't know. I care for you. I don't want to hurt you. All I want to do is talk—as we used to. As we did last year, when talking to you seemed to be the easiest thing on earth and now seems so difficult. Impossible almost.'

'Nick—' she began again, but before she could continue there was a knock on the door and Ruth Mathews, the receptionist on duty, entered.

CHAPTER TWO

Erin gazed out on the scene before her. The Minster tower hid the early morning sunshine, casting shadows onto the cobbled lane below. The market-place was busy with tourists, so easy to define amongst the locals—cameras slung across chests, maps at the ready. Erin could hear the bustle of the traders setting up their stalls. She loved this time of the morning—the little town beginning to come to life, the excitement of market day and the cry of gulls overhead, attracted from the sea by the sight and aroma of the food below.

She turned from the balcony window and went into the bedroom, frowning into the long pine mirror that stood beside her large double bed. She had put on a sleeveless pale green dress for work this morning. It was too warm for tights or stockings but her naturally olive skin had deepened its tone to a smooth, summery tan.

Adding a dash of perfume behind her ears and slipping on white high-heeled sandals, she felt ready to start the day. Saturday morning surgery was shared equally among the four doctors—Alissa, Max, herself and now Nick.

She felt a strange sensation of unease when she thought of the resident living in the flat below her. Luckily, their conversation had been interrupted by Ruth yesterday. She didn't want to be rude to Nick, but there was no way she was going to haul through the events of last year.

After Simon, she had learned an important lesson. She had trusted completely—something she would find hard to do again. She had been so sure of him and to suddenly discover that she had been living in a dream . . . no, she wasn't eager to make that mistake again.

It was the real world for her now, concentrating on her career and, yes, a change of direction. London after Christmas—and why not? She still had friends there, her old circle of contacts. Perhaps she had become disenchanted with City life, before moving to Hayford Minster, but that was a long time ago now. Her dreams of country life with her perfect husband had long since faded . . .

Erin turned quickly away from the mirror. She didn't want to think about Simon—or Nick Hanson. Today she would take the early surgery then shop around the market for an hour or so. Tomorrow she intended to catch up on her letter-writing. The family back home in Dublin would be wondering how she was. It was high time she let them know about her move back to London, she told herself firmly.

Picking up her case and bag, she locked the flat, hurried down the stairs and let herself out into the lane. It was cool and pleasant in the shade of the old buildings. The mews cottages were just coming to life—doors opening, curtains being drawn.

Juggling her case and bag in one hand, she unlocked the car and slid in. Once belted in, she pushed the key into the starter and flicked it. An ominous chugging sound filled the lane. She twisted it again, with the same result. Then a funny little clicking sound came from within as she tried yet again.

'Trouble?' someone asked beside her.

She jumped, turning to find Nick standing beside the car, peering in at the open window. 'Oh, Nick—er, yes.'

'Battery?'

She nodded. 'I think so.'

'I'll check the terminals, but it sounds flat.'

'Are you sure? Have you time?' She glanced at his arms, full of fresh vegetables and fruit. He wore a T-shirt with a Vancouver logo and navy blue Bermudas, with a pair of sturdy thongs on his tanned feet.

He lowered the packets of fruit and vegetables to the doorstep, then turned his attention back to the car. 'You didn't leave your lights on last night, by any chance?'

Erin felt the colour flood into her cheeks as she glanced down at the switch and realised that she had. 'I can't believe I left it with the side lights on,' she mumbled vaguely.

'Easily done but, don't worry, it's mendable,' he called. Going to the bonnet, he lifted it and peered in.

'Well, there's nothing wrong there, as far as I can see,' he told her a few minutes later. 'I expect the battery needs charging. It will take a little while, but I'll drop you in to the surgery, then come back and see to it.'

'That's really not necessary—' Erin began, only to be stopped as Nick opened her door, grinned and gestured, not towards the hired saloon car he had been driving but to a dark green BMW parked on the other side of the lane.

'I collected it from the distributors yesterday,' he told her, as he lowered the bonnet. 'It could do with a run-in.'

Erin realised that she was in no position to refuse. Though she would be able to walk to the surgery in a few minutes, should there be an emergency she would be without a vehicle. So, accepting the offer, she found herself being driven to work as Nick carefully negotiated the narrowed lanes that wove around the town centre.

'It would be best to leave your battery on charge for a couple of hours at least,' he told her as she settled back into the smooth leather seat of his new car. 'I shall be at home, so ring me if you need me for any reason. Is Max on call today?'

She nodded. 'Yes, it's his weekend on call.'

'So, other than any emergencies that arise at the surgery, you'll be OK?'

Again she nodded. 'Look, this is very good of you Nick, but—'

'I'll collect you at half eleven. That should give you time to finish.'

'That really isn't necessary. I'll walk.'

He said nothing as he pulled up at the surgery, but merely smiled, watching her as she climbed out.

'See you later, and thanks.' She closed the door of the car and watched him drive off. He stuck one tanned elbow on the lowered window, raising his hand as he drove away. Erin collected her thoughts as best she could then turned and walked towards the L-shaped cottages that had once been used as a craft centre. The whitewashed buildings, with their fully equipped treatment centre, five consulting rooms, offices and comfortable waiting areas had been open as a clinic for eighteen months now.

Max and Erin had joined Alissa and Alec Rogers to make the modem town-centre location a popular practice. Erin had loved working here and as she walked into the low-beamed reception room, she realised again how much she would miss it.

'Hi, Dr Brooks!' Keeley Summers, the youngest of the reception staff, smiled at her.

'Hello, Keeley.' Erin glanced around at the waiting area and crèche, noting that two young women were sitting there. 'Sorry I'm a little late. The car wouldn't start. Are these two people waiting?'

Keeley nodded. 'One's a temporary resident. The other is a permanent patient. A Mrs Pauline Ford.'

At once Erin recalled who it was and, going to her room, she reflected on what Nick had told her yesterday about the problems within the Ford family. Seeing first the temporary resident, a holiday-maker who had a summer cold and nothing more, Erin then smiled at Pauline Ford who was shown in by Keeley.

'Mrs Ford . . . how can I help you?'

The small, attractive-looking woman with short blonde hair took a seat. The records showed that she was thirty-one and a PA within a large electronics company based near the town.

'I'm not sure,' Pauline Ford said quietly. 'You see, six months ago I separated from my husband. Our little girl lives with him. I can't have her because we are living in temporary accommodation—a one-bedroom flat. I'm hoping to move soon, but Marina, who is six, becomes upset when I leave her. She spends the weekends with me but I'm coming to dread Sundays and returning her home. I feel very depressed. Could you give me something to help?'

Erin gave her a brief physical examination which revealed no physical problem as far as she could discern. Pauline explained that she had met and was now living with a man six

25

years younger than herself.

'He's not terribly good with kids,' she explained hesitantly as Erin removed the rubber cuff of the sphygmomanometer, 'so at weekends he goes out with his friends.'

'And there's no hope of a reconciliation with your husband?' Erin asked.

'Even if Mark and I split up, I don't know if it would work with Des.' Pauline looked away. 'We've had problems before, although I've never been unfaithful to him in ten years of marriage. Not until I met Mark.'

Although she didn't mention the rash that Marina was exhibiting, Pauline said she was concerned about her daughter's reaction to her affair with Mark. Erin realised that she was an intelligent woman who was aware of the distress her relationship was causing. However, the underlying message was that the marriage had been in difficulty before the younger man had come on the scene.

Erin prescribed an antidepressant, explaining that it was not a cure to the real worry from which Pauline was suffering. She also suggested that some form of counselling might help, independently from Desmond. Reluctant to agree, Pauline did, however, make a follow-up appointment for a few weeks' time.

*   *   *

As Erin left the surgery at half past eleven, a green BMW came to a halt outside the practice. 'I thought you might like some lunch,' Nick called as he pushed open the passenger door.

'I was going to do some shopping at the market,' Erin protested, but found herself sinking into the leather seat. 'You shouldn't have bothered, Nick. It's only a short walk.'

'It's no trouble.' He indicated to turn into the road again, glancing in his driving mirror. Erin saw that he had changed his clothes and now wore casual trousers and a light-coloured sweatshirt. 'Where would you like to go?'

'I'm really not hungry,' she said, glancing at her watch. 'And I should get home.'

'Have you something special to do?'

She wished she had, but there was nothing. 'Not really.'

'Well, then, sit back and relax.' He grinned at her. 'Don't worry, I'll have you back before nightfall.'

She had to laugh at this and, seeing her amusement, he laughed, too. As he drove out of the town he explained that her car was now in working order, and she thanked him. Almost without knowing it, she found herself falling into conversation.

The day was glorious, bright July sunshine and a light breeze. He drove steadily and soon Erin realised that they had taken the motorway and were now heading towards the

New Forest.

'Like old times,' he said quietly, and glanced at her.

She smiled uncertainly, making no reply. And though she hoped that they were not about to visit the same place as they had last year, Nick turned off the motorway and took one of the leafy roads that wove into the heart of the Forest.

'Thirteen months,' Nick mused, 'but it seems like yesterday.'

'Nick, I would prefer it if we didn't—'

'Look, there it is,' he interrupted her, and, pointing to a lane on the right, raised his eyebrows. 'The same place, but under new management, apparently.'

Erin glanced at the large but discreet sign that stood on the roadside. The Briar House Hotel was indeed described as being under new management. Nick was peering ahead and Erin's heart beat faster as the hotel came into sight, reminding her of the day they had spent here thirteen months ago. However, nothing much had changed on the outside, the elegant gabled building with its leaded windows and timbered walls looking just as lovely as it had before. Perhaps more flowers spilled from the baskets and troughs and maybe the white walls gleamed a little brighter in the sunshine, but otherwise all remained the same.

Nick stopped the car and, leaning on the steering-wheel with his arms crossed, he looked ahead, scanning the building. 'Nothing much has changed,' he said quietly. 'I'm glad of that. I hoped we'd find it as we left it. It's good to know that some things are exactly as you remember them.' He turned his head and looked at her, his eyes dark with meaning.

Erin looked down into her lap. 'Nick, why have you brought us here?'

'Isn't that obvious?'

Erin shook her head slowly. 'Nick, there's no point in going over the past.'

'I don't want to,' he said huskily. 'I want to stay very firmly in the present. I want to make a new start, Erin, but to do that we have to remember what we shared together. I want us to be honest about what happened last year.'

She looked up then. 'There was nothing, Nick—'

'There was something,' he corrected her, turning in his seat, 'something that we shared, and you know it, Erin, but you're not willing to admit it. You weren't then, and obviously you aren't now.'

'I was about to get married,' she protested, her lips trembling as she stared at him.

'That made no difference—' he held her unsteady gaze '—to what was going on between us.'

'We went out together a couple of times,' she argued weakly. 'We had a meal here and talked as friends. We enjoyed each other's company. That's all there was to it.'

'Not for me,' he told her quietly. 'Erin, I was deeply attracted to you. You must have known that.' His eyes would not let hers go.

She found herself silently shaking her head, her feelings so confused she couldn't bring herself to speak. Was there an element of truth in what he was saying? Had she known that there was an attraction between them and refused to accept it?

'Simon wasn't the man for you,' Nick said as she gazed wordlessly at him.

'You hadn't even met him,' she breathed, unable to believe she was allowing herself to be provoked into this conversation. 'We'd been together seven years. Simon wanted what I wanted. We had planned a future together—'

'*You* had planned a future,' Nick said, and raised an eyebrow. 'It was your dream, Erin, not his. Otherwise he would be here, sharing it with you.'

'That isn't fair,' she answered, angry now, taking in a sharp breath of air. 'Simon was the only man—' She stopped, embarrassed, her cheeks flaming. Then, as tears pricked her eyes, she looked away. 'Please, take me home,' she said unsteadily.

For a few seconds he merely stared at her and, although she refused to meet his gaze she could feel his eyes seeming to burn her skin through the wing of chestnut hair that had shielded her cheek.

Eventually he turned back and reached

for the ignition key. The next thing she heard was the engine bursting into life, and she looked out of the side window as he drove slowly down the lane. Her eyes misted again as memories of the past forced themselves through the mental barricade she had erected. Why had she allowed Nick to do this to her? After all this time, trying to rebuild her life, a few hours spent in his company had forced her to confront issues that she had carefully laid to rest.

Was what he said about her true? Had she really been attracted to him in that way? And, if that was so, what did that say about her feelings for Simon?

They drove back through the beautiful afternoon and the silence deepened between them as they neared home. The questions tumbled through Erin's mind as though a tap had been turned on in her brain and, try as she might, there seemed no way now to stop it.

*   *   *

A week later, Erin had little doubt that Nick had decided to leave her alone. When they passed in the corridor or met in the office or staff room he was polite but distant, his manner making it plain that he had got the message.

As it was her weekend on call, she was kept busy with visits. Briefly passing him on Sunday morning as she left the flat, they greeted one another but didn't stop to speak. Which was why, that evening, when Alissa phoned her, Erin found their conversation so difficult.

'Godmother?' Erin repeated in surprise as Alissa took a breath.

'I can't think of anyone else I'd rather have as a godmother for Jake,' Alissa told her. 'Max has no close relatives. That's why I'd hoped that you and Nick would say yes.'

'Nick?' Erin was shocked, and knew she sounded it, immediately trying to disguise her reaction.

'I phoned him this morning,' Alissa went on. 'Have you seen him? Did he say?'

'Er . . . no.' Erin was reluctant to admit that, out of the surgery, they avoided each other.

Alissa hurried on. 'The christening date is convenient for him—the first Sunday in September. Would it be for you, Erin?'

'I'm not sure . . .' Erin bit her lip. 'What about the call duty?' She tried to recall exactly whose duty it was, hoping it was hers.

'Alec is going to locum for us,' Alissa explained. 'That means if you've no prior arrangement for three o'clock, we're all free. I hope you'll say yes, Erin.'

'Well, I—' Erin tried to think of a plausible excuse and knew that there were none. She was touched that Alissa had asked her, but if she were to be godmother and Nick godfather, that obviously meant . . .

'There are just a couple of meetings beforehand,' Alissa said apologetically. 'Very short, just for the record, as it were.'

'I see.' Erin hesitated. Before she could say more Alissa was thanking her, explaining that she would let her know more of the details later.

Erin sat for some while afterwards, reflecting that there was no way she could have politely refused. And why should she? She was flattered and honoured at the request.

*   *   *

It was as Erin hurried downstairs the following morning that she bumped into Nick. At the precise moment she opened her front door he opened his.

As had happened before, they both spoke at the same moment. Nick smiled, his dark eyes moving over the soft pink summer suit she wore and her freshly shampooed hair, falling in soft, glossy waves around her face. 'You know, one of these days we are going to have to get our act together,' he said, arching an eyebrow.

She nodded. 'Yes, I suppose we are.'

As they walked together towards the cars he said, 'I heard from Alissa over the weekend.'

'Yes, I did, too.'

Nick hesitated. 'And you've agreed to be a godparent to Jake?'

Again she nodded. 'As you have.'

He was silent for a moment, then lifted his shoulders as he turned to face her. 'Erin, I would rather move than have this atmosphere between us.' He looked down at the pavement and shuffled a stone with the tip of his shoe. 'In fact, I phoned the landlord and explained that in the next few weeks I would probably be looking for somewhere else to live.'

Erin was shocked. 'But that isn't necessary, Nick.'

He looked at her. 'No? Surely it's better I move than wreck what remains of our friendship. You've made the situation clear. I accept it. And in view of Alissa's request, the answer, I think, is for me to find alternative accommodation.'

She opened her mouth to protest, then realised that what he was saying was perfectly true. She had gone to great lengths to avoid him—had glanced out of the window many times to see if the BMW had been there, had left earlier than necessary on some mornings, had arrived home later than she normally did.

As though she suddenly saw how childish her behaviour seemed, she also understood that for some reason it had to do with her fear of facing her feelings towards this man. She didn't want to ask herself why. She had gone to all these lengths to keep him at arm's length—and what for? Why? To avoid talking about Simon? To avoid unhappy memories?

34

Or was it that she was scared of admitting other truths? Truths she didn't want to accept because they were too painful, too unpleasant and, most of all, too revealing?

Nick was staring down at her, his eyes full of concern as she tried to compose herself. At seven-thirty on a beautiful summer morning she was about to burst into tears.

'I—It's all right, I'm OK,' she mumbled, swallowing hard and blinking rapidly.

'Erin, this is the last thing I wanted to happen—'

She nodded, stepping back, out of his reach. 'Yes, I know.'

'What have I done?' He shook his head in bewilderment. 'Look, I'll go. I'll leave . . .' He stepped hesitantly into the lane but Erin shook her head, stretching out a hand as she blinked again through the mist covering her eyes.

'Nick, don't go,' she quavered as she cleared her throat. 'I'm s-sorry for being such an idiot.'

He stood still, his tall figure dressed impressively in a dark shirt and trousers, his deep brown cap of hair catching the first rays of sun that reflected from one of the mews' windows. He looked confused and worried and Erin took a hesitant step forward. She managed somehow to compose herself and, looking up at him, she said, 'I've been extremely rude. I apologise. There's no reason for you to move from the flat.'

'It seems the only alternative.' He shrugged.

'I don't want to live here, knowing that you are finding my presence—'

'I'm not,' she interrupted guiltily. 'I'm happy that you've moved in and the place is being used again.'

As a cyclist passed them they moved to one side and he stepped towards her, reaching out to lay a hand on her arm. 'I hope we are still friends.'

She nodded. 'Of course.'

His expression was still concerned. 'I'll see you at the surgery, then.' Pausing for a few moments, he met her gaze, and as she smiled he returned it. Then, without saying more, he walked to the BMW.

Watching him drive away down the cobbled lane, Erin took a tissue from her bag and blew her nose. She couldn't pretend to understand what was happening to her, but she knew one thing for certain. She didn't want Nick to move from the flat because of her and she would be mortified if he did so.

Neither of them referred to the incident again, but Erin was aware that the tension between them had lightened and that on the occasions they met they were more relaxed with one another. The week was extremely busy, though, the temporary residents claiming more attention than ever before, possibly because of the good weather.

The following week, a young man walked into Erin's surgery whom she recognised immediately. The hour had been set aside for emergencies to be seen by the duty doctor, and most of these were usually visitors to the area. However, this morning it was Mathew Sibson who entered.

'Mathew, how are you?' she asked as he lowered himself slowly into the chair.

'Not so good, Dr Brooks, I'm afraid.'

Erin studied the twenty-eight-year-old, noting his painful movement. She glanced at his records and saw that his previous visit had concerned a broken arm that he had sustained while rally-driving. Last year she had treated Mathew for two other breaks, fractures to ribs and wrist, sustained because of his love of fast cars.

'It's whiplash this time,' he admitted reluctantly. 'Ten days ago, I was hit by another car and came off the track at a bend. I was unconscious for a bit. Hurt my knee, head and neck.'

'You were taken to hospital?' Erin asked as Mathew rolled up his jogger leg.

Mathew nodded. 'Couldn't remember a thing until I woke up in the ambulance.'

Erin gently examined his swollen knee. 'There's still fluid here,' she explained as Mathew winced. 'It's manufactured as part of the body's defence system. They took X-rays, of course?'

He nodded. 'Nothing broken. I think they were more worried about the time I was out.'

Erin stood up and frowned. 'And you're moving your head with difficulty?'

'Whiplash, I think.' The young man lifted his shoulders carefully then dropped them with a sigh. 'To be honest, though I've had breaks before, I've never felt so bruised and battered. I just feel like my whole body is tender and aching. Even turning my neck is painful. And I've been getting these headaches.'

Erin looked at Mathew's inflamed shoulder muscles and realised that he must have absorbed a much greater impact than he remembered. 'Well,' she sighed, 'you'll be out of action for a while, I'm sorry to say. When is your next race?'

'In two months. It's a big rally. The best of the year.'

Erin sat down and met his gaze. 'I would be very surprised if you were ready for it. I think you should consider at least six months for a full recovery.'

Mathew shook his head. 'No way, Dr Brooks. I must get fit.'

Erin decided she wouldn't argue with him at this point. Instead, she suggested that a course of physiotherapy was in order, plus some assistance with pain control and the inflammation. 'I'll give you some painkillers, Mathew.' She printed out the prescription and handed it to him. 'You may find you'll want something a little stronger. If so, come and see me again.' She smiled. 'Don't worry about the knee. The fluid will gradually clear, but for now, I'm afraid, my advice is to rest. Your body has taken a big shock. Allow it to recuperate.'

'Not exactly what I needed to hear, Doc,' complained the young man as he eased himself into an upright position. 'And don't you start telling me I should pack it in. I've had enough of that from my girlfriend. On about it the whole time, she is.'

Erin refrained from commenting that he was fortunate to have sustained only minimal damage over the years. Fast cars were Mathew's obsession; she knew that he would never consider giving them up.

'I'll get the physio to look at you as soon as possible,' she told him as she saw him out. She watched him walk slowly and stiffly down the corridor then turned as voices came from the office. Alissa, accompanied by Nick, walked towards her. Erin was aware that Nick was staring at her and as Alissa began to speak she saw that he stood a few feet back, watching her.

'So if that's all right?' Alissa was saying.

'Oh . . . yes,' Erin replied hesitantly. Dragging her thoughts back, she realised the subject was Jake's christening.

'Wonderful,' said Alissa. 'Max and I will look forward to it.'

'Look forward to what?' Erin asked uncertainly when Alissa rushed off.

Nick frowned at her. 'Aren't you aware of what has just been arranged? We've been asked to go to the Minster on Saturday.'

Erin nodded. 'Yes. Alissa mentioned there may be several meetings . . .'

Nick arched an eyebrow. 'And afterwards?'

Erin looked at him blankly. 'I'm sorry, I'm not with you.' She stared at him, knowing that whatever it was he was about to tell her she wasn't going to like it one little bit.

CHAPTER THREE

'We're having dinner—making up a foursome with Max and Alissa,' Nick explained, his dark eyes studying her face. 'To be honest, I couldn't think of an excuse either.'

Erin shook her head. 'I wasn't concentrating . . .'

'I could see that.' Nick thrust a hand through his hair and threw her a glance. 'Unless either of us can think of a reason why we shouldn't go, I'm afraid we're stuck with it now.'

Erin nodded. 'Yes, I suppose we are.'

'Anyway,' Nick said abruptly as he moved to the door, 'I must go. I've several calls to make before lunch. One of them is to Marina Ford.'

Erin looked up. 'Is it the rash problem?'

He shook his head. 'No, Ruth said that

when she took the message Desmond explained that his daughter had a temperature and sickness—possibly the bug that seems to have been circulating at school.' He paused. 'I don't suppose you've thought any more about speaking to her mother?'

'I already have,' Erin said. 'Oddly enough, she came in to see me recently, though we didn't discuss Marina. The problems within the family are complicated.'

'You mean there's more to it than the other party involved?'

'Of course,' Erin replied shortly. 'It's hardly fair to lay all the blame at Pauline Ford's feet.'

Nick frowned. 'I hadn't intended to. It's just that Desmond has said very little and I'm trying to treat their daughter, who is obviously the victim of her parents' conflict.'

Erin realised that they were both in a difficult position regarding the Fords. She and Nick weren't on opposite sides—they should be working together as one to help this family who seemed to be at a loss to help themselves.

'I've asked Pauline to come and see me again,' she said quickly. 'I've suggested counselling, independently of her husband.'

'Do you think that's likely?'

Erin shrugged. 'I'm not sure. When we talk next perhaps I'll have a better idea. At the moment she's rather defensive about the whole thing. I don't want to alienate her, but should there be an opportunity to speak about

Marina, I'll take it.'

He nodded slowly. 'OK. Thanks.' He paused, then said a brisk goodbye and went on his way, leaving Erin to ponder on the problem of the Fords and how best to help. Instinctively, Erin felt that the relationship Pauline had struck up with the younger man was not all that she had hoped it would be.

Returning to her room, Erin gazed out of the window, and from behind the blinds watched Nick unlock his car. He looked tall and handsome in his dark suit, and for a moment Erin caught herself wondering what had happened to Sherry Tate, the woman with whom he had been involved in Canada.

Alissa had told her that the relationship was over. Was this the reason he had returned to England? From what he had divulged last year, their lifestyles were conflicting—Sherry's was high-profile, while Nick's was more low-key. They had met while he had been involved in a series of medical programmes for Canadian radio. Was he still getting over Sherry? she wondered.

The BMW flashed past the window and Erin returned to her seat. She attempted to concentrate on the paperwork lying on her desk, but found that her thoughts—seeming to have a life of their own these days—returned to Nick.

*   *   *

Erin gazed up at the stunning fifteenth-century medieval glass window which had been assembled by Flemish craftsmen. She was acutely aware of Nick's presence beside her as they waited for the Darvills under the fresco roof of the Hayford Minster choir vestry.

The sun shone through the glass in a kaleidoscope of colour, sending soft beams to filter down onto the glossy dark wood of the pews.

'It's a magnificent building,' said Nick in a low voice. 'So much light and colour.'

'Yes, it's beautiful,' Erin agreed as they stared at the pastoral scene depicted on the windows, attempting to focus her mind not on the past but firmly on the present.

'But you must have mixed feelings about the place,' Nick murmured as he looked down at her, reading her thoughts.

She nodded, swallowing. 'I did at first. But I'm over that now. And I like to come here and just sit sometimes.'

It was true, though, she did have mixed feelings about the Minster. It was here she had arrived one lovely day in the summer of the previous year, her wedding gown swirling around her ankles, the fine silk skimming the tessellated pavement of the porch as she'd stood waiting for Simon, her fiancé.

Her hand had been firmly around her father's arm. Her heart had been

43

beating rapidly as she'd gazed in at the congregation, waiting to see her. Those minutes of expectancy had slowly changed to apprehension as she'd waited and then to desolation and confusion as the minutes passed by and Simon hadn't appeared.

'Are you all right?' Nick asked her softly, breaking into her thoughts.

'Yes, I'm fine,' she said, despite the cold shiver that ran over her neck. 'I didn't want this place to hold bad memories,' she said a little shakily as she looked away. 'It's so much a part of my life in Hayford Minster. I look at the tower every morning from my balcony, I watch the sun sink behind its silhouette. So I came here soon after my family went back to Ireland. I felt I had to.'

The first visit hadn't been easy. She had called in one day after work and had sat in one of the pews, quietly determined to face the awful memory of the vicar explaining that there would be no service. The groom had telephoned to say that he'd been unable to attend.

How could Simon have been so cruel? She had asked herself this a thousand times afterwards. How could he have abandoned her like that? How had it been possible for two people to have got to such a point in their lives and then have it destroyed?

Simon had never been able to give her a satisfactory answer. And what answer would

44

have justified not turning up for your own wedding? She had been forced to accept his feeble explanation, that he could not bring himself to commit to such a step and had decided that, even though he had hurt her and humiliated her, it had been best in the long run. He loved her, he had protested, but he also loved his life and career in the City.

Erin looked up at Nick and found him frowning at her. 'I'm sorry, Erin.'

She shrugged, her body cool under the tailored pink suit. Unlike her wedding dress, the material was cotton and summery, cut to a modern style around her slender body.

She was five feet seven inches tall and in her high-heeled shoes this morning she gained another two inches. Despite this, she had to crick her neck to look up into Nick's dark gaze.

'We're meeting them in the christening chapel.' Erin abruptly changed the subject. 'We had better go or they'll think we haven't arrived.'

He nodded, though he was slow in turning, and walked beside her down the aisle towards the thirteenth-century tower to which Erin had referred. Their steps echoed on the ancient stone and Erin breathed in the scent of history, strangely combined with Nick's own particular aroma, tangy and smooth as it was brought over on the cool currents of air.

Alissa and Max had arrived with their family and Alissa smiled, her face radiant. Max's two sons, Bas and Aaron, stood with Sasha, Alissa's daughter from a previous marriage. Baby Jake, in Alissa's arms, gave a tiny gurgle as Erin stepped forward to kiss her on both cheeks.

Max fell into quiet conversation with Nick as they waited for the minister to arrive. Aaron, tall and handsome at almost sixteen, stood by his father, as the two younger members of the family went to explore the Minster. Although Bas was two years older than eight-year-old Sasha, they had formed a close friendship, one which had helped to cement Max and Alissa's relationship.

When the minister arrived they all gathered in the tiny chapel. Erin stood beside Nick, watching the delight of Max and Alissa and their family as they assembled around the ancient font. Erin's heart gave a small pang.

This was what she had imagined for herself and Simon. What she had dreamed of. A man with whom she could have shared the rest of her life. Here, in a town she loved and worked in, carving out a future she had created in her dreams as a little girl.

For a moment emotion overcame her as the minister explained the responsibilities involved as godparents. She felt Nick listening intently beside her and she wondered if he was thinking of Sherry.

Almost as though he had caught her thoughts somehow, he glanced at her. For a

46

moment their eyes met and Erin swallowed, aware that his smile was warm and tender and that his eyes were a deep, rich brown, so dark and fathomless she didn't want to look away.

* * *

'Max said eight for eight-thirty,' Nick explained as they stood in the lane, after leaving the Darvills at the Minster, 'so we'd better leave around seven-thirty.'

Erin nodded. 'Yes, all right.' She took her key from her bag. 'Do you know where the restaurant is?'

'Yes, not far. A little village called Tolleybridge. A place named Splinters. Do you know it?'

She shook her head. 'I'm afraid not.'

They stood for a while, not speaking. After the intimate moment in the Minster when their eyes had met, Erin had felt oddly disorientated. Her response to Nick had affected her. How, she wasn't quite sure, but it was only now as she stood here that she realised she had stopped thinking about Simon from that moment and had been absorbed in the present, more aware of the man beside her than of her unhappy memories. Something, she felt, had changed in that moment, though she was at a loss to know what it was.

Nick was looking down at her. 'See you later, then?'

47

She wanted to ask him up for a drink, felt that it was only polite to do so, but then she thought better of it, and as he was already entering the door to his flat she quickly opened hers.

The afternoon stretched before her and she decided to take a shower, wash her hair at leisure and find something to wear that would be appropriate for the meal at Tolleybridge. She hadn't thought to ask Alissa what she was wearing that evening but, assuming that it would be a dress, she searched her wardrobe and selected several dresses, each of which she decided were wrong for one reason or another.

On impulse, she pulled on jogger bottoms and a T-shirt. In ten minutes she had jostled her way through the market stalls and arrived at a small boutique which, she had noticed, had recently opened. As luck would have it, what she chose took her no more than a few more minutes to try on and she was back at home within the hour.

The dress was not one she would have normally chosen. It was expensive and made of silk—a pure luxury. It was also the soft green shade of her eyes. Luxurious and sexy, the smooth material fitted her slender curves perfectly. It was classically styled and stated the fact. The neckline was low but subtle, two delicate straps weaving their way across her tanned shoulders. The hemline stopped just above her knees, the waist was tailored and the

48

pencil-slim skirt was broken by a back slit that allowed her full movement. With high heels it was a dream.

By seven o'clock that evening, Erin had stopped trying to convince herself that she wasn't trying to make an impression. She was, and she had better acknowledge the fact. The dress was not for her benefit alone and Erin was self-consciously thinking about that as she lifted her hair and wondered whether to pin it up. No, that looked too austere. It also looked overstated. With her hair falling into a smooth bob around her ears, the ensemble was complete.

By seven-thirty she was as nervous as a kitten. And by the time Nick called for her she was trying to convince herself she wasn't shaking. She just hoped Nick wouldn't notice. When she opened the door her fingers trembled on the lock.

He smiled as she pulled it back, the smile fading as he stared at her. His eyes travelled over her and it was evident he was taken aback. In a husky voice he said, 'Erin, you look lovely.'

'Thank you.' She was so nervous that even her voice seemed to shake.

'Are you ready?'

'Yes.' She lifted her small black bag and slid the slender strap over her shoulder. On legs that felt like cotton wool, she walked with him to the BMW. He had dressed in

49

a light-coloured suit, a dark shirt and tie complementing this. His tall figure took the modern style well, and as he opened her door for her there was that familiar lick of electricity between them that made her swallow and slide onto the leather seat with her heart pounding.

Very soon they had left Hayford Minster and were travelling out towards the hills that lay under a feathery white haze of heat. The August colours in the evening sunlight were dazzling—yellow and green fields tumbling over themselves, dotted with sheep and cows, the lazy grey road ahead of them winding over the landscape like ribbon.

They said very little and Erin knew that they were only talking to avoid a silence that might envelop them. She sensed they were both equally nervous. She felt strange yet elated, and her heart had still not slowed from the anxious pace that had gripped it as she had opened the door to him. The excitement was growing inside her and she could not deny it.

Max and Alissa arrived at the restaurant soon after Nick and Erin. The hotel was famous for its cuisine of fish dishes, fish reputed to be caught locally in the river that flowed through the village.

The table was set on a balcony overlooking the river, and the first course of a consommé was delicious. The grilled trout and fresh vegetables ordered afterwards slid down perfectly with the smooth French wine.

During the meal Alissa and Max kept up the conversation with anecdotes of the children, thus dispelling any tension that had been in the air. Alissa looked blooming, Erin thought, dressed in a pale peachy-coloured trouser suit that complemented her creamy complexion and ash-blonde hair. She had regained her petite figure after the birth of Jake and it was evident that their marriage was a success.

After the delicious caramel sweet, they went to the cloakrooms, before joining the men in the bar. Gazing into the mirror, Erin saw that she was flushed, and Alissa noticed, too.

'Is that a new dress?' Alissa asked as they stood before the mirror.

Erin nodded, her cheeks flushed as she tried to avoid Alissa's perceptive stare. 'Yes. Do you like it?'

'It's gorgeous,' Alissa said admiringly. 'It's about time you splashed out on yourself, you know.'

Erin turned to face her friend. 'It's been a lovely evening. I've enjoyed myself.'

'You've worked very hard since I left to have Jake,' Alissa replied. 'I know it's been a difficult year for you . . .'

Erin nodded, looking down at her bag and carefully closing the clip. 'I haven't attempted much of a social scene, I'm afraid.'

'Have you heard from Simon lately?' Alissa asked cautiously.

Despite the feeling of disquiet her

ex-fiancé's name engendered, Erin shook her head. 'No, we've not been in touch.'

'He never really explained his reasons to you for what happened that day?'

'Only that he couldn't bring himself to take the final step.'

'Not much to go on,' Alissa said wryly, and Erin smiled, managing to see the lighter side. After a short pause she asked, 'How are things between you and Nick?'

That was the one question Erin had been hoping to avoid. 'To be fair, we don't see a great deal of each other except at work,' she answered, quickly wondering if her brisk tone would be enough to halt further enquiries.

But Alissa wasn't to be deterred. 'I don't know if Nick has told you this, but his relationship with Sherry broke up because she met someone else—had, in fact, been seeing him for quite a long time,' she said as she gazed into the mirror and applied a dab of powder to her cheeks.

'I had no idea,' Erin answered hesitantly. 'How awful.'

Alissa's brows knitted in a small frown. 'Apparently, Sherry had been seeing this colleague at work. Nick discovered the affair when some mutual acquaintance decided that he should be told.'

Erin frowned. 'Is that why he left Canada?'

'I think Sherry may have been one of the reasons,' Alissa said as she turned to smooth a coat of lipstick over her lips. 'Nick has said very little to us about his private life. The last time we really talked was on the telephone earlier this year when he decided to accept our offer of a partnership.'

Little more was said of Nick and Sherry as the two women repaired their make-up and combed their hair, their conversation digressing to children and to the christening in September. Finally they walked back to the bar where Max and Nick were waiting for them. They were both tall, handsome individuals, and for a moment Erin took a breath as the two men turned to smile as they approached. Her eyes, though, were only on Nick as he stood up, pulled out a high-backed stool and helped her up onto it.

She studied him as they sat and talked, wondering how he had felt about Sherry's deception and how it had influenced his decision to return to England. Quite suddenly she realised that she was no longer preoccupied with thoughts of Simon and that she was enjoying being with Nick.

She began to recall the moment last summer when he had taken her home after their day out and had bent his head to kiss her goodbye. Instinctively she had raised her mouth to his, knowing at once there was a strong and powerful connection between them.

'Time to go,' Max said after they finished the coffee, which had been served at the bar.

'Mrs Dunphy isn't as energetic as she used to be, I'm afraid. No doubt Bas and Sash will have kept her occupied with their homework for the best part of the evening.'

Once again Erin realised she had been miles away and, catching Nick's amused gaze, she found herself thankful for the shadows of the evening as they walked out to the cars.

It was a beautiful, star-filled evening, and as they said goodbye to Max and Alissa Erin was aware that she didn't want the evening to end. On the return journey to Hayford Minster the road was lit by a full moon, casting bright shadows across their path. There was little traffic in either direction and Erin felt a pang of disappointment as the BMW approached the familiar outskirts of town.

As they drove into the lane, Nick threw her a glance and smiled. They had exhausted most subjects throughout the evening, and as the engine died he unclipped his belt, looking up at her flat.

'Well, that wasn't too painful, was it?' he asked, turning to her with a grin. 'Home before midnight and still in one piece.'

She laughed. 'I enjoyed the evening. Did you?'

He nodded. 'Very much. Is it too late to ask you in for a drink? A nightcap? A coffee? Something even less potent?'

She shrugged, smiling. 'Why not?'

For a moment he looked surprised, then,

climbing out of the car, he came around to open her door. 'I wasn't prepared for company. I'm afraid the place is in rather a mess. I had some things shipped over from Canada and they arrived yesterday.'

'Won't you want to get on with unpacking them?' she asked as they arrived at the two front doors.

'It can wait until tomorrow,' he said as he inserted the key into the lock.

Once inside the flat, with the lights switched on, Erin saw that he hadn't exaggerated when he'd said the place was in a mess, although on closer inspection she found there was order in the chaos. Two small packing cases were placed on two larger ones and a number of articles lay on the carpet, a bin full of wrapping paper at one side.

'I sold virtually everything before I came over,' he told her as he turned on the low lighting around the room and extinguished the main overhead lights. 'These are just one or two pieces that I decided to keep.' He gestured to the long, low white sofa that spanned a wall on the other side of the room. 'Take a seat. What would you like to drink?'

'Oh—tea, I think.'

'Tea it is.' He disappeared into the kitchen, a room to the right, but instead of sitting down she remained where she was, staring at a half-opened package. There were two or three small articles on the floor and one of them appeared to be a small photo in a silver frame.

Bending down, she saw an attractive woman with very short, dark hair, dressed in shorts and a T-shirt, standing at the helm of a boat. In the background, Nick was looking out to sea, his tall figure attired in the same casual dress.

She was so intrigued that she didn't hear Nick come up behind her. Then, sensing his presence, she looked up. 'She's very beautiful,' Erin said softly. 'Is it Sherry?'

He nodded. 'Yes. Taken a couple of years back. She was a keen sailor.'

'And you?'

'Yes, I suppose you could say so. Come and have your tea.'

Erin stood up and followed him to the sofa. When they'd sat down and he'd handed her a cup, she frowned. 'Tell me about her,' she said quietly.

He was silent for a moment then shrugged. 'I told you last year more or less everything there was to know. The fact is that her career—and mine to some extent—made our relationship . . . tenuous.' He smiled vaguely. 'I'm not sure that's quite the right word.'

'You said last year that there were long separations.'

He nodded. 'Sherry travelled a fair bit. She was good at her job. The cable network she was with was expanding.' He shrugged again. 'We saw less and less of each other. Then the inevitable happened and she met someone within the company.'

Erin nodded slowly. 'That must have been a shock for you.'

'Not really. As you know, last year our relationship had come to an impasse.'

'Because of the other man?'

He shook his head. 'In retrospect, no. We went to Italy after I left England and spent some time actually talking. The oddest thing was, neither of us had a great deal to say.'

Erin frowned. 'But you were together for a long time . . .'

'Five years,' he said quietly, then added, 'Five years to discover that neither of us had very much in common, that our goals were entirely different and that whatever it was that had been the attraction in the early stages had long since disappeared.' He paused and, sitting forward, rested his elbows on his knees, smoothing his finger around the rim of the coffee-cup. 'Do you remember last year when I asked you what you really knew about Simon?'

Erin felt the familiar tightness in her stomach. 'Yes, I remember.' She looked away from his swift glance. 'You have every right to say that you warned me.'

'I'm not saying that—'

'Simon wanted what I wanted,' she broke in tersely. 'Or so I thought.'

'A life of rural bliss?'

She did look at him then. 'What was wrong

57

with that?'

'Nothing, from your point of view.' His dark eyes raked her face. 'It was *your* dream Erin. Simon went along with it and found himself unable to speak up.'

'So you were at pains to tell me last year,' she said, standing up, gripping the mug of tea she hadn't finished drinking. 'I think I had better go now.'

'Do you always run away when confronting personal issues?' he said, and rose, too.

'I just don't want to talk or think about Simon,' she said sharply, and glanced down at the photograph on the floor.

Nick followed her gaze and, taking the mug from her hands and lowering it to the coffee-table, reached towards her, bringing her firmly against him. 'Sherry was part of my life,' he told her, his voice husky. 'And I'm not about to say that I wasted five years of it. I learned a lot in that time and I don't intend to sweep any of it under the carpet as though it was worthless.' He tipped her chin up to force her to look at him. 'However, I realised that I wanted . . . needed . . . a lot more than Sherry could ever give me or I could give her. And thank God, we hadn't arrived at the point of making vows . . .'

'Don't—' Erin began, her body shaking as he refused to release her.

'Don't what?' He looked into her eyes and frowned, his dark eyes glimmering. 'Don't
58

refer to what we shared in those few weeks last year and so dispel the fantasy you have of your relationship with Simon? Don't make you remember that when I kissed you there was something special between us? Does talking about this make you realise that even then you knew that you and Simon were wrong for each other, but that you wouldn't—or couldn't—admit the truth?'

'Nick, that's unfair!'

'No,' he said challengingly, his voice a low whisper, 'it's perfectly fair. And I'm going to prove it to you.'

As her mouth opened on a soft gasp, he bent his head, his lips coming down over hers, his tongue flicking out to explore the sweetness within and his hands bringing her firmly against his chest so that there was no escape.

CHAPTER FOUR

Erin closed her eyes and felt the weeks and months falling away until she recalled the taste and pleasure that had swept through her the year before as Nick had kissed her, the kiss she had chosen to forget even though her response to it had touched on the truth of the relationship she'd shared with Simon.

Now Erin was brought to the full realisation

of what had happened. As Nick's arms tightened around her, her hands went up and around his shoulders, her fingertips brushing his hair. Her body seemed to have a mind of its own as she shuddered against him, his tongue seeking her response.

She didn't try to protest for that would have been a lie, too. She had wanted Nick to kiss her all evening, hadn't she? She'd stared across the table at him as he'd talked, his full, firm mouth revealing the familiar flash of white teeth as he'd smiled. As their kiss deepened she swayed, his hands supporting her, the heat generated between them like a slowly burning fire.

She didn't know how long the kiss lasted. It was only when she realised that they were still in each other's arms as the Minster clock chimed that she moved away, pushing against him with the palms of her hands.

'Don't go,' he said in a soft voice, holding her wrist. The chemistry between them was undeniable as he bent his head to one side, his voice husky as he stared at her. 'Stay, Erin.'

As she hesitated her eyes fell on the packing cases that stood to her right and the photograph in the silver frame that lay on the floor. The attractive face of Sherry Tate looked up at her, and with a sudden dart of pain at her ribs she wondered what Nick's real feelings were towards his long-term partner.

'It . . . it's late,' she heard herself mumble

as she moved away, then walked to the door. 'Goodnight, Nick,' she breathed shakily, and, lifting the latch, she slipped out, inhaling deeply as she stepped into the night.

Once in her flat she hurried up the stairs, went into her bedroom and sat down on her bed. Making an effort to control her erratic breathing, she realised that she had wanted to stay with Nick, had wanted to remain in his arms.

How could that be so, she asked herself, when her thoughts had been so preoccupied with Simon since their parting? She had been in love with Simon, had never wanted another man. Simon had been her one love—and until last year the man she had planned to marry.

With an effort, she pulled herself to her feet and began to slide off her dress. The smooth material slipped easily between her fingers as she hung it in the wardrobe and closed the door.

For a moment she stood there as Sherry Tate came once more to mind, her large, dark eyes staring out confidently under the elfin cap of ebony hair. It was then that Erin realised the dart of pain she had experienced had been a moment of jealousy, and with a start she asked herself once more how that could possibly be so.

*　　　*　　　*

The following Monday Erin arrived at work with the intention of ignoring what had happened on Saturday evening; there was too much at stake to allow one evening to upset the equilibrium at work. Much as she reasoned that neither of them had set out to allow things to get out of hand, the fact was that it almost had.

Both on the rebound from long-term relationships, Erin had decided that Sherry Tate still had a place in Nick's heart. His explanation that he had no intention of denying the events of the past hardly accounted for having Sherry's photograph—and his—shipped over from Canada, and it appeared to be one of the first items he had chosen to unwrap.

A five-year relationship wasn't dismissed in five minutes. She herself could testify to this. She had met Simon while training, and they would have celebrated their sixth anniversary this time last year.

As Erin tried to settle into the morning, she attempted to put thoughts of the weekend behind her. By twelve-thirty she had completed her surgery and was about to leave her desk for a brief lunch in the staffroom when the telephone rang.

Ruth Mathews said, 'It's Dr Hanson on the line, Dr Brooks. He asked if you were free. Is it OK to put him through?'

'Yes, go ahead, Ruth.' Erin waited for the

sound of Nick's voice, her heart giving a small rush as Ruth connected them.

'Erin, I'm on the last of my visits,' he said briefly. 'At the Fords' house.'

'Is it Marina?' she asked.

'No, it's your patient, Pauline Ford. I wonder if you could call over here right away? Suffice it to say I want to admit her to hospital. I think it might well be an ectopic pregnancy. However, she is very distressed and is refusing to go. It would help, I think, if you would speak to her.'

Erin glanced at her watch and calculated that she had an hour free before the start of her afternoon surgery. She didn't know why her patient was reluctant to go to hospital but if Nick was correct in his diagnosis it meant that there was no time to spare.

'Do you think you can call?' he asked again.

'Yes, I'll be there directly,' she agreed at once. After saying goodbye, she hurriedly collected her things together, before leaving.

It took Erin less than ten minutes to arrive at the Fords' large house, an attractive detached building in a quiet avenue. The garden was cultivated with shrubs and flowers, a drive sweeping around the back of it. The general appearance of the place said much of its owners, people who cared about the property they lived in and worked hard to maintain it. Pauline Ford had revealed that she was living in temporary accommodation with her lover and Erin found it difficult to imagine how she could accept those circumstances in comparison to the home she shared with Desmond.

It was an impression that persisted when Erin walked in to find herself surrounded by tasteful décor and antique furniture. Nick had left the door ajar and Erin called out, aware there was movement from upstairs.

Nick appeared at the top of the long flight and, stepping down several stairs, gave a small signal. 'Mrs Ford is up here,' he called. He wore a short-sleeved white shirt and dark trousers, and as she grew closer he said in a lowered voice, 'She's lying on Marina's bed. The child is at school and her husband at work. It's the room at the end of the corridor,' he added briefly.

Erin nodded and followed him along the wide hallway, glancing in at the bedrooms as she passed. Each of them was large and bright, fitted with thick-pile carpeting, the muted colours giving a general impression of wealth and comfort.

Inside Marina's bedroom a single four-poster bed dominated the floor space. The light pine furniture and soft drapes made it plain the room was a girl's, and there was a lavish selection of toys and teddy bears on the surrounding cupboards.

Pauline lay, fully dressed, on Marina's bed. Her neatly styled blonde hair was damp with perspiration and she was clearly distressed.

Nick stood back for a moment, then spoke. 'I'll wait downstairs,' he said quietly. Picking up his case, he walked out of the room.

'Hello, Pauline,' Erin said, and sat down on the chair that was pulled up beside the bed. 'Now, what's happened?'

Pauline looked up at her, her face bathed in perspiration. 'Dr Brooks, I don't want my husband knowing and Dr Hanson is Des's doctor. I'm so worried he'll find out—' She drew in a sharp breath and placed her hand over her stomach as her body shook with a spasm of pain. 'I . . . I can't believe that I'm pregnant, I just can't,' she whispered hoarsely.

'Let's have a quick look,' Erin said gently. She leaned forward and lifted Pauline's blouse, moving down her skirt top and palpating her abdomen in order to identify the area of pain. She also checked the blood pressure and pulse rate and discovered that both were above normal. Pauline's temperature was raised and, in conjunction with this, she complained of nausea.

'How long have you been in pain?' Erin asked as she put her patient's clothing back in order.

'It . . . it began in the night. I had to get Marina back home this morning for school. She needed her uniform. Mark hasn't got a car so I caught a taxi. I can hardly remember the journey, I felt so ill. Des was at work, thank

65

goodness. Our daily help was here and she took Marina to school for me. I just said that I had an upset stomach. Couldn't it be that? Couldn't it be a gastric problem?'

'No, I don't think so, Mrs Ford,' Erin said, and shook her head. 'When was your last period?'

'I missed last month, but that happens sometimes with me.'

Erin raised her eyebrows. 'Well, I have to say that I agree with Dr Hanson that the chances are this may be an ectopic pregnancy. It may not be but, either way, we have to get you into hospital for investigation.'

At this, Pauline Ford bit her lip and closed her eyes, eventually nodding as a small tear escaped from between her lashes. 'I have to go back to the flat. I have to tell Mark.'

'Can he be reached by phone?' Erin asked.

'We're not on the telephone in the flat,' Pauline said wearily. 'And the public one downstairs has been vandalised.'

'Well, let's take first things first and get you to hospital. As Dr Hanson has probably explained, if you are pregnant and have an ectopic pregnancy it means the foetus isn't growing in your womb but in one of your Fallopian tubes—'

'Mark will be worried,' her patient interrupted as tears filled her eyes. 'He might think I've decided to . . . to . . .'

Erin pulled a tissue from a box on the

nearby set of drawers and handed it to her weeping patient. Giving a small sigh, she said, 'If you like, I'll call and tell your friend, but it won't be until after I finish my surgery.'

'Would you? Oh, thank you, Dr Brooks.' Pauline bit her lip as tried to compose herself. 'His name is Longman, Mark Longman.'

Erin nodded and went downstairs just as Nick was about to use the telephone in the hall. 'I'm dialling the hospital,' he said quietly. 'Agreed?'

'Yes, agreed. It's probably an ectopic, though it might be an ovarian cyst . . .'

'But you'd guess at an ectopic?'

'Either way, she'll have to go in.'

Erin listened to Nick on the telephone and wondered why Pauline was so concerned about her husband discovering the pregnancy. It seemed to be distressing her more than anything, and as Erin returned upstairs and walked into Marina's bedroom she could only draw the conclusion that Desmond's probable reaction—whatever it might be—was the reason.

'The ambulance won't be long,' Erin explained as she drew near the bed.

Pauline looked up at her, brushing a tear from her cheek. 'Mark and I had an argument over Marina last night. I want us to move into a larger place and Mark is content to stay at the flat, but there's no room to have Marina. He doesn't seem to realise how much I miss

67

her. Th-that's why he might think I've come back to Desmond.'

Erin was aware that her patient seemed more concerned about Mark than he appeared to be about her, but she refrained from remarking on this.

Before long the ambulance had arrived and Pauline was safely aboard it and on her way to hospital.

Erin and Nick left the house and returned to the surgery, both having afternoon surgeries. It was after five-thirty when Erin was able to telephone the hospital and enquire after Pauline who had, it transpired, been taken to Theatre during the afternoon.

Leaving the surgery, Erin drove to the temporary address she'd taken from Pauline's notes and parked her car outside the Victorian house on the outskirts of town, which had been divided into flatlets. Erin stood in the shabby porch and selected the bell push for flat number four. Pushing it several times, she was about to turn away when the door opened.

'Mr Longman?' Erin asked the young man who stood there in jeans, no top and bare feet.

'Yes, that's me. What is it?' The tall, dark-haired young man frowned at her as she explained who she was and why she had called.

'You'd better come up, then,' Mark Longman said after a few moments. 'I'll get some of Pauline's clothes. Will you give them to her?'

Erin was taken aback by this. 'Won't you be going to the hospital to see her yourself?'

'I can't this evening,' he said quickly. 'I work then.'

Without asking any more questions as to Pauline's welfare, Mark led the way up the narrow stairs and into a flat on the first floor. As Erin had begun to realise from the moment she'd drawn up outside the house, there was no comparison to the comfortable home which Pauline had given up for her lover.

Mark disappeared from the room and Erin waited, studying the cramped flat. Other than a large television and hi-fi system, the only item of furniture in the room was a large leather settee.

Returning quickly, the young man handed her a rucksack. That's all I could find,' he said dismissively, and walked to the door and opened it.

'Is there a message you'd like me to give her?' Erin paused on the landing outside.

'Just that I'll get in to see her when I can.'

For a moment Erin couldn't believe what she'd just heard. She wondered how Pauline could have considered a future with a man who was so patently disinterested in her welfare. As he stared at her, she realised that waiting for him to ask any further questions about the woman who had shared his life for the last few months was a waste of time. Without saying more, he turned away to leave Erin to stare at the closing door.

When she arrived back outside, she looked back up at the flat and wondered what was lacking in Mark that he could display such disinterest in his partner and make no effort to support her during this difficult time.

Erin walked to the car, painfully aware that although the circumstances had been different in her own case it had taken an aborted wedding ceremony to wake her up to the reality of her own unhappy plight the previous year. With a shiver going down her spine, she hoped that Pauline wouldn't leave it too late to face the truth of her unhappy situation and somehow avoid the heartache that seemed inevitable for all the Ford family.

*   *   *

Erin didn't stay long at the hospital that evening when she took the rucksack to Pauline. Just recovering from the emergency operation to remove part of a Fallopian tube, she wasn't well enough to receive visitors. Erin did, however, leave word with the nursing staff and wrote a small note which she left in the rucksack.

Thoughts of Pauline persisted, but by the time she went to bed Erin had decided that there was little more she could do. Becoming involved in the family drama would serve no purpose, especially at this point when Pauline was so adamant that her husband should not be told of her state of health.

The following day Erin saw Nick and explained what had happened, though his only remark was to say that he hoped he wouldn't be confronted during the week by Desmond Ford and Marina. That was a possibility, Erin realised, and wondered what would happen at the weekend when Pauline normally had her daughter to stay.

The problems of the Fords had at least made a contact point between her and Nick, and Erin was thinking of this when, later in the day, he knocked on her door. 'This might seem rather odd, but I've just been talking to a patient who has given me an idea for a gift for our godson.'

For a moment Erin hesitated as she realised Nick was referring to Jake. She frowned. 'I hadn't actually thought about anything yet,' she murmured.

'Me neither,' he acknowledged, walking towards her. 'But we shall have to start looking for something, won't we?'

Again Erin hesitated. 'Yes, I suppose we will. But is there any rush?'

Nick shrugged. 'No. However, this idea might take a little time.'

Erin frowned, then couldn't resist a smile. 'This sounds very mysterious.'

'Not at all,' Nick said with a grin, 'but I think you'll like what I'm going to suggest.'

71

At that point Keeley came up behind Nick and arched an eyebrow. 'One late emergency, Dr Hanson. Can you see a boy of fifteen with a sore throat? Says he's got a school virus. Sounds to me as though he's chesty, too.'

Nick nodded and took the records Keeley handed him. When she had gone, Nick looked back at Erin. 'Would you mind if I called around later this evening to discuss it? It will be easier in the long run. I'll only keep you a few moments.'

'I'm on call,' Erin said quickly, then added as she saw the disappointment in his face, 'But I'm sure I can find a half an hour to spare if it's about Jake.'

'You won't be disappointed,' he told her.

As he smiled at her and disappeared, whistling a little tune as he went on his way, Erin realised she had done exactly what she had promised herself she wouldn't do. She wanted to avoid the familiarity that living so close might engender. Habits were hard to break. And after the other evening, especially, she wanted to start as she meant to go on.

Working with Nick was one thing, but seeing him socially was another. She wasn't ready for an affair. She wasn't ready for any kind of commitment after Simon, and she was quite sure that Nick wasn't either. Whatever he said about Sherry, Erin was sure that she was still in his thoughts, just as Simon was in hers.

Then another thought sent colour flowing to her cheeks as almost instantly she realised her mistake. Simon was rarely in her thoughts these days. When the memory of last year occasionally flashed through her mind, she was able to dismiss it quickly. No, if she was honest, Simon was a shadowy figure, unlike the mental picture she had of Nick and the way he had looked at her the other evening when he had taken her in his arms and kissed her. Was it this that frightened her so much? Was this the real truth? That she could find herself so strongly attracted to someone other than Simon?

She smiled grimly, the irony not lost on her. For so many years she had devoted all her affection to Simon, had been devastated when he had abandoned her on their wedding day. Yet now she couldn't take her mind off Nick Hanson—a man she had only met for a few weeks last year and who now was causing her all this consternation. It just didn't make sense.

*   *   *

Her phone rang at eight-thirty that evening. She thought it was a call for a house visit and answered it with a rush of relief that she would have a genuine excuse to get out of the flat and avoid seeing Nick.

But her heart fluttered as she heard the familiar voice. 'Erin, could you come down here?' he asked. 'You'll see why.'

'I'm on call,' she reminded him, only to realise that protesting was useless. She had her pager and, when activated, the alarm would alert her wherever she was. Her excuse sounded pathetic and she added quickly, 'Give me a few minutes, then. But I really can't stop.'

'Yes. I know that.' His reply was untroubled.

As she took her keys from her bag and took a brief look in the mirror, smoothing back her hair and checking her make-up, she wondered what it was that Nick wanted. She'd believed him when he'd said it was about a gift for Jake, but she had vaguely assumed that they would buy their own christening gifts. They were not a couple and they were acting as independent godparents to Jake, as confirmed by the vicar who wanted only the reassurance that each of them had Jake's spiritual welfare at heart.

So what was she doing? she asked herself as she locked the flat and knocked on Nick's door. The answer flashed into her mind as it opened and Nick stood there. He wore a cool-looking sweatshirt and a pair of tan pants, his dark hair smoothed back from his face and looking slightly damp as though he'd just showered.

Her heart raced and she felt a wave of pleasure—or possibly anxiety—as she returned his smile. Why couldn't she tell the difference? All she knew was that he made her feel like this—a shower of goose bumps flowing over her skin, a small pulse drumming somewhere in her head as blood rushed through her ears.

'Come in.' He grinned and she stepped into the flat, now completely transformed from the last time she had seen it. The leather settee was now partnered by a pair of sea-green leather recliners, and there were thick multicoloured rugs on the floor. Books filled a wall on one side and a section was given to music, a library of cassettes and CDs beneath the system. The packing cases had vanished but a neat pile of photos and albums lay on a glass-topped coffee-table.

'The room looks lovely,' she said as her eye caught a shape in the comer. 'What have you got there?'

He took her elbow, gently steering her towards what appeared to be a large white artist's canvas. He reached over to switch on an uplighter beside it and, manipulating the stem of the light so that the glow reflected on the canvas, he arched one eyebrow. 'Do you like this?' he asked as he gestured to a large colour print attached to the top right-hand corner of the canvas.

Erin stepped forward, narrowing her eyes. 'It's Alissa and Max and the children,' she said in surprise.

Nick nodded. 'I took it shortly after I came over.'

'It's beautiful, Nick.' Erin saw that Nick had captured the whole family perfectly. Aaron and Bas were sitting on high stools behind Max and Alissa. Baby Jake lay in Alissa's arms, his tiny fist coming up to wave in the air, and Sasha, sitting at her mother's feet, had lifted her hand to rest on Jake's tiny foot. The Darvills were dressed informally, which gave the photograph added appeal, and Erin found herself for the moment without words.

'It was rather a fluke, the way it turned out, because I hadn't bothered much about lighting,' Nick said modestly, 'and when one of my patients—who's an artist—happened to be talking about his work today, an idea sprang to mind. I asked him if he could reproduce a photo like this in oils on canvas and he said he could.'

'That's a wonderful idea,' Erin agreed. 'Has he seen the photograph?'

Nick shook his head. 'No, but he's confident he can do it. He had several canvases in his car and gave them to me to show you in order to get some idea of size. I said I would discuss it with you and we would let him know. Of course, I explained that you might have something else in mind.'

Erin shook her head as she gazed at the photograph. 'No, I hadn't given a gift much thought yet. I think it's a lovely idea. The photograph is perfect—have you an interest in photography?'

Nick shrugged. 'My preference is black and white studies. I like to experiment with light and dark.'

'I didn't know that,' Erin said softly. 'Do you develop your own prints?'

'As a rule, yes, but I've had to put most of my stuff in the boxroom for now. I'm afraid the contents of those packing cases took up more space than I bargained for. Anyway, what do you think? Fergus has left his price list and other info with me, though the cost will depend on how large the picture will be.'

'Are they the other canvases?' Erin asked as she nodded towards a selection of white boards propped up by the bookcase.

'Yes, I'll show you.'

Time sped by as they talked, and as the Minster clock chimed ten Nick asked her if she would like a coffee before she left. She agreed, though she realised they had been deep in conversation for well over an hour.'

'May I have a look at your work while you make the coffee?' she asked, and he shrugged.

'If you like.' He gestured to the hall. 'You know the way. I'm afraid it's still pretty disorderly in there but help yourself.'

Erin walked along the narrow hall to the small room she knew was on the right. In her own flat she used this as a spare room for visitors, but Nick had chosen to fill it with packing cases, some of the contents of which were placed around the room.

Much of his equipment was stacked neatly on the shelves, a large selection of lenses and cameras lined up neatly beside each other. She knew little about photography herself but she knew enough to know that Nick's interest in his hobby was keen, as the large portfolio cases were to reveal.

There were prints inside of Canada, of vast areas of forest and sea and several of cities. They were impressive scenes that revealed a beautiful country, and she gazed at them in fascination, opening the pages and studying the material which was a record of Nick's former life.

Just before her pager activated she lifted a large album from the shelf. In time with the alarm of the instrument clipped to her belt, a rush of adrenaline sped through her body as she gazed down at the beautiful woman to whom the book appeared to be dedicated.

Sherry Tate's smile was pensive, her large eyes expressive. She was seated at a desk behind the logo of a broadcasting company. She wore a dark suit and she gazed at the camera confidently, obviously at home in the atmosphere that surrounded her. The study was in black and white, the shadows cast expertly across the poignant scene. Nick had taken the photograph with instinctive skill, revealing the essence of the woman with whom he had once shared his life.

Swallowing, Erin closed the book. She replaced it on the shelf—and turned to find Nick watching her, a mug of coffee in each hand.

CHAPTER FIVE

'I heard your pager,' Nick said quietly.

Erin nodded, colour flowing into her cheeks. She removed the small device from her belt and studied the information on its screen. Looking up, she said, 'I'm sorry, but I don't think I'll have time to drink the coffee.'

He shrugged. 'It doesn't matter.'

She moved past him, gesturing vaguely. 'You're very talented,' she said quickly. 'You've taken some lovely photographs.'

Without replying, he accompanied her to the door, placing the two mugs on the glass table. 'You're happy for me to go ahead and confirm with Fergus?' he asked her as hc opened the front door. A warm breath of air filtered in, bringing with it an unmistakable scent of summer.

'Yes, as far as I'm concerned, that's fine,' Erin agreed at once.

'I'll let you know what he says and when we can expect the painting to be finished,' he said softly, his eyes on her as she stepped out into the dusky night.

'Yes, all right.' She hesitated, then, glancing back at the mugs on the table, said lamely, 'I'm sorry to rush off.'

He smiled resignedly. 'It comes with the job, doesn't it?'

As she drove to the house visit she thought about Nick and Sherry and felt that strange sensation under her ribs as she did so. Was their relationship really over, she wondered, or was Nick doing exactly what he had accused her of—running away?

Why did it matter so much anyway? Why was she so upset to discover Nick had taken such beautiful photographs of the woman he once loved, or still did love? Last year, when they'd discussed their lives in that brief time they'd spent together, she hadn't felt this way. They had talked about Simon and about Sherry objectively—so what had changed? Why was she feeling this way?

Erin shook her head as if to clear the thoughts away and as she pulled up outside the block of sheltered housing flats she looked for the main entrance. It was here that she would find Gladys and Tom Knight, both of whom had taken tumbles, according to the warden. Putting all thoughts of Nick from her mind, Erin parked and pushed the bell of flat twenty-two and gained entrance.

Tom Knight had suffered from low blood pressure for years and his circulation was poor. As he had fallen, his wife had come to his rescue only to fall herself. Fortunately the red bell-string was at hand and the warden had arrived within minutes.

'I don't remember what happened,' Tom said bleakly as he sat on the edge of his bed. 'My legs just went underneath me.'

'He doesn't remember anything at all these days,' said his wife, who sat in a chair opposite. 'He's getting very depressed. And so am I. I'm having to think for two all the time.'

'I don't want to go to hospital,' announced Tom as Erin examined the grazing on his head and legs. 'You never come out of those places. I've seen it happen to my neighbour. He had a bad memory and they carted him off, never to be seen again.'

Erin smiled. 'I don't think you'll have to worry about that, Mr Knight. Luckily you're in good shape. Just shaken.' Erin turned to his wife. 'Now, how are you, Mrs Knight?'

'It's my hip,' Gladys said, and winced. 'I've seen the doctor about it before, but after the fall it really aches.'

Erin examined her and studied the notes that Max had made, suggesting the necessity for a hip replacement in the near future.

'Have you heard from the hospital yet?' Erin asked.

'No. Not a word.' She looked at her husband. 'And with him the way he is, I couldn't leave him anyway.'

'Well, we'll see what we can do,' Erin said as she examined Gladys, satisfying herself that there was no fracture. 'I'll chase up the hospital and ask Social Services to call. I'm

81

going to give you something for pain relief, and your husband's cuts and bruises will be a little painful tomorrow, but there's no long-term damage done.'

'Thank you, Doctor.' Gladys frowned at her husband. 'Memory's a precious thing. We take it for granted, but when we can't share our memories our lives are lacking, I'm sad to say.'

They were words which Erin recalled as she drove home. Nick had said something very similar when he'd talked of the past and its bearing on the present. She thought of the Knights and guessed that they had shared many years together. At least they had one another.

She looked up at her darkened flat as she parked the car and, then at Nick's window and wondered if he was still up. Was he thinking of Sherry? Did he miss her presence in his life? Did he yearn to see her again?

With a sigh, Erin climbed out of her car and, after locking it, paused as she stood in the street. Some crazy notion made her want to tap on Nick's door and for a moment she was tempted. But then the moment passed and she slid her key in her lock, closing the door quietly behind her.

*   *   *

On the following Tuesday, Alec Rogers put his head around Erin's door. 'Everything OK?' he grinned. 'Time for a quick chat?'

'Alec—come in. It's nice to see you.' Erin got up and walked over to the doctor who had once been senior partner at the practice, but who these days enjoyed life in retirement, spending much of his time on his beloved boat. She kissed him on both cheeks and he gave a chuckle.

'That was worth coming in for,' he teased her. Taking a seat, he removed the jaunty little cap that covered the somewhat untidy thatch of iron-grey hair. 'How are you, Erin?'

She nodded. 'I'm fine, thanks.' She laughed softly as she sat down. 'I don't have to ask how you are, Alec. You look wonderful.'

'Thanks to Aggie, the love of my life.' He lifted rueful, bushy eyebrows. 'And the wife, of course.' *Agatha* was the name of Alec's boat. He always spoke in glowing terms of her to the amusement of everyone because they knew Alec was a devoted husband and adored his wife. 'Thought I'd come in to fix up the fortnight's work,' Alec went on. 'Kirstie wants me in on the last Monday of August through to September.'

Erin nodded. 'The weeks before school starts. It's usually bedlam.'

He laughed. 'The kids manage to restrain their colds and flu to the very last day of the holidays. Still, don't blame 'em. Can't say I was too keen to get back to the grindstone when I was younger.'

83

'Well, it will be nice to have you back here for a bit,' Erin said sincerely. 'Like old times.'

'Talking of which,' Alec said in a quieter tone, 'Alissa tells me you're thinking of leaving after Christmas.'

Erin nodded. 'Yes, I am.'

'I'm sorry to hear that.' The older doctor frowned. 'Not happy here in Hayford?'

Erin hesitated. 'I've been very happy, Alec. It's just time to move on, I think.'

'It will be darn difficult to replace you,' he sighed. 'You've built up quite a following. Kirstie got anyone up her sleeve yet?'

'She hasn't mentioned it to me,' Erin admitted as she recalled her last conversation with the practice manager, Kirstie James. 'But it's early days yet.'

'Quite. Well, I must let you get on.' Alec made to stand up, his energetic body almost leaping out of the seat. But to Erin's horror he suddenly went white and fell forward onto her desk. The chair toppled over behind him and his body shook as he tried to steady himself.

Erin was beside him in an instant and he leaned heavily on her. She couldn't have supported him for much longer and was relieved when she heard someone come in. She looked up to see Nick's arms sliding under Alec.

'It's all right, I've got him.' Nick took the other man's full weight and Erin bent to pick up the chair. Soon Nick had lowered him carefully into the seat, but Alec's face was grey. His right hand came up to his chest and Erin and Nick glanced at one another anxiously.

'I'm OK, it's all right,' Alec told them breathlessly. 'It'll pass. It always does.' He sat back in the seat and took a breath, the colour slowly returning to his face. After a few seconds he looked up at them and said, 'Sorry about that.'

Nick frowned. 'How long has this been going on, Alec?'

'Not long,' said the older doctor. Sighing, he pulled back his shoulders as he tried to take a breath.

'What are you doing about it?' Erin asked quietly as she took out her stethoscope and listened to Alec's heart.

'Nothing, at the moment.'

Alec breathed out slowly and as Nick drew up a chair all three doctors were silent as Erin made her examination.

After she had returned to her desk Alec said, 'Before either of you say anything, I know it's time to sort it out. I've just been putting off the evil day—as most of us do.'

'Is there a family history of heart problems?' Nick said levelly, and Erin knew that he was taking a guess at Alec's problem, but by the expression on the older doctor's face there was no doubt that Alec was aware of what was happening to him.

'I'm afraid so,' Alec acknowledged. 'My

father and grandfather had angina and I seem to be having similar problems. My father lived, however, until his nineties.' Alec's tone was dismissive. 'I'm quite sure that I'll carry on for a long time yet.'

'I'll arrange some tests for you,' Erin said firmly. 'No doubt you've been putting them off.'

Again Alec nodded. 'There's so much to do on the boat and, besides, I didn't want to worry my better half.'

'You'll worry her a lot more if you keel over in front of her one day,' Nick observed.

'You're absolutely right. I've said it to my own patients dozens of times before, but admitting to it myself isn't quite so easy.'

'We'll begin with an ECG right away,' Erin said referring to the technique used to detect structural and functional abnormalities of the heart. 'And go from there. Until we've a better idea of what's going on, Alec, I suggest you take things a little easier.'

'Yes, I know the ropes,' Alec said with a weary smile.

Erin made arrangements for the diagnostic test as Nick talked to Alec and soon after that the older man left. Nick frowned at Erin as he paused, before following Alec out.

'You've not completed surgery yet?' he asked, glancing at his watch.

'No, just one more patient to see, I believe.' Erin glanced at her list and saw the name of a temporary resident with whom she wasn't familiar.

'I've some information from Fergus Brown on the portrait. He's given me a few sketches to show you—I have them in the car. What about something to eat at the Lady Jayne and we can discuss it then?'

Erin hesitated. The Lady Jayne was the small hotel where she and Nick had first got to know each other last year. They had enjoyed several snack meals and had talked of their lives, finding one another's company easy and companionable in the little restaurant of the market square hotel. 'Well . . .' She hesitated. 'I'm not sure if I've any calls . . .'

'I've checked and there's just two, both Max's patients.'

'Oh.' Erin realised there was nothing to stop her and she wondered why she was hesitating. 'All right, then,' she agreed. 'I should be finished by six.'

'Great,' Nick said, and smiled. 'See you at the cars.'

Erin nodded as her last patient was shown in. As the door closed, she collected her thoughts and listened to the holiday-maker's complaint, a summer cold that had resulted in a chest infection. Prescribing the relevant antibiotic to relieve the problem, she then completed the small pile of prescriptions to be signed, answered the queries left by the reception staff during the day and finally gathered her things.

She had worn a light calf-length summer dress in denim, and she was pleased to see that it hadn't creased as she glanced at her reflection in the long cloakroom mirror. Repairing her make-up and brushing her hair into a glossy brown bob, she felt she was ready to meet Nick.

Saying goodbye to the evening staff, she walked out into the warm August evening, reflecting that she was looking forward to Nick's suggestion of eating out. She wouldn't have bothered normally, and on Tuesdays she often met a friend at a local squash club in order to relax. However, tonight she had made no arrangements, and when she saw Nick standing by the BMW, just locking it, her heart gave a flutter of excitement as he smiled.

'Shall we walk?' he asked as she approached, tucking a slim folder under his arm. 'It seems too nice to drive.'

Erin nodded. 'Yes, we can cut through to the square by the river path. Are they the sketches?'

Nick nodded. 'They're pretty good. All we have to do is select the one we like and Fergus will begin the painting.'

They set off together, and as Erin had suggested, took the cobbled walkway past the buildings that flanked the practice and led to the banks of the little river that flowed through Hayford Minster. The sun glinted off the fast-

88

flowing water and hundreds of tiny fish swam with the current. Ducks and swans gathered at the banks, some of the tourists feeding them. Many of the cafés and restaurants had gardens leading down to the river banks and the Lady Jayne was one of these, originally a coaching hotel with stables and a courtyard at the rear.

As they entered the foyer, Nick stopped to allow another couple to move past them. The young man limped awkwardly across the floor then stopped. 'Hello, Dr Brooks.' For a moment Erin didn't recognise him until he added, 'It's Mathew—Mathew Sibson.'

'Oh, Mathew—hello.' She saw that he was accompanied by a young woman who stood slightly to one side.

'This is my fiancé, Gemma.' Mathew turned stiffly and gestured to the slim young woman in jeans.

Erin smiled. 'Hello, Gemma.'

The girl nodded but said nothing, and there was an awkward pause before Mathew said politely, 'Are you eating here?'

Erin explained they were about to go to the restaurant, but stopped in mid-sentence as another group of people arrived and Gemma waved and went over to join them.

'That's Gemma's family,' Mathew explained hurriedly. 'Oh, by the way, I'm starting some hydrotherapy next week. I hope it's going to help. The physio said it would ease the whiplash and help the knee.'

'I'm sure it will,' Erin said, who already knew this from the notes the practice physio had made.

'Well, I'd better go,' Mathew said as Gemma glanced back at him, her expression impatient. 'It's a bit of a celebration tonight. Gemma's dad wants me to go into the family firm and I've decided to accept. It'll mean a steady job and career prospects, but I'll have to give up rallying.' He shrugged resignedly. 'So I'm not so worried about getting fully fit for next month's race.'

'Does that mean you'll be giving up racing altogether?' Erin asked.

'I suppose it had to come,' Mathew responded quietly. 'I couldn't really expect Gemma to understand how I feel about racing. I'll just have to try to forget about it and concentrate on an ordinary job.'

Erin smiled. 'Well, enjoy your evening, Mathew.'

When he had gone, Erin glanced at Nick. 'He's a young rally driver,' she explained as they made their way to the restaurant and found a table. 'And he's had one or two rather nasty injuries, the last of which seems to have made him think twice about the sport.'

'The girlfriend doesn't approve?' Nick queried.

'No, he said that she didn't.' Erin picked up the menu, not really concentrating. She looked at Nick who was staring at her. 'I'm astonished that he's given up his racing career—it was his whole life, despite the injuries.'

'Family pressure, no doubt,' Nick commented.

'Do you think so?'

'What else could it be?' Nick was frowning. 'The girl's father is offering him a job, no doubt trying to steady him down for his daughter's sake.'

'Yes, I suppose that stands to reason,' Erin said distractedly.

Nick was silent for a moment then tilted his head thoughtfully. 'The adrenaline rush is obviously what he lives for, though. It's going to be tough, getting that kind of excitement out of his system—if he ever does.'

Just then the waitress arrived and they ordered, but Erin found herself preoccupied as they sipped ice-cold mineral water. As they looked at each other across the table Nick smiled ruefully. 'Your sympathies lie with the girl and her family, don't they?'

Erin frowned. 'As a matter of fact, I'm not altogether sure now. They would have once, but . . .'

'But?' Nick prompted.

Erin shrugged. 'It's not up to me to pass an opinion, Nick. I'm just his GP, dealing with his medical problems.'

'But you do have an opinion?'

She nodded. 'Yes, I do.' She looked down at her fork, turning it over several times before raising her eyes to meet Nick's again. 'If you must know, I don't think marriage is the answer for Mathew Sibson, or the day job with the career prospects. I think he's going to regret giving up his rallying and regret it bitterly.'

Nick sat back and as their seafood entrées were served he watched her, his eyes not leaving her face. 'You sound as though you're speaking from experience,' he said once they were on their own again. 'Has what you've just said got any bearing on what happened to you last summer?'

Erin took a breath and knew that it did. Perhaps all along she had known that she had been asking Simon to give up too much. Had she been as blind as that young woman who had stood in the foyer of the hotel and beckoned to her fiancé, unaware just how much of a sacrifice she was asking him to make? Had Simon been so desperately unhappy about his decision to leave the City and move to Hayford Minster that it had gradually driven a wedge between them?

'If we didn't learn by experience,' she said as she sat forward and picked up her fork, 'then how could we hope to help ourselves or our patients? However, it won't be for me to bring up the subject with Mathew. Perhaps love will prove to be all the adrenaline rush he needs.'

Nick smiled, his eyes filled with amusement. 'Perhaps it will,' he said softly, 'just as long as

92

it's the right love that he's chosen.'

The meal was excellent and, with Mathew Sibson forgotten for the moment, the conversation centred on Alec. Neither of them felt happy about the older doctor's reluctance to have tests for his angina, nor did they feel that Alec was taking his condition as seriously as he should. But once they had finished their meal of delicious roast chicken garnished with herbs, followed by a light caramel sweet, they adjourned to the lounge bar and sat and studied the sketches provided by Fergus for the oil painting.

They chose one which had been given a slightly contemporary feel and decided on a size that would sit neatly on a fireplace wall. Ending the evening with coffee, it was almost nine by the time they emerged from the Lady Jayne, their arrangements complete.

'Would you like to come up?' Erin asked as they walked home towards the Minster. 'I can make some cool nightcaps, if you like, and we can sit on the balcony and drink them before it gets dark.'

'I'd like that,' Nick said quietly. 'I'll leave the sketches in my flat first, then come up directly.'

They arrived in the lane and Erin gestured to her door. 'I'll leave it on the latch, so just give it a push,' she told him, her heart fluttering as he smiled at her.

She hurried upstairs and opened the

93

windows on her balcony, trying to calm her emotions. Why was she feeling so nervous? And what on earth had possessed her to ask him up to her flat?

Taking some ice from the freezer, she broke it into glasses and topped them up with fruit juice and a dash of white wine. As she placed them on the balcony table she heard the click of the front door latch and Nick's light footfall as he ascended the stairs.

Fortunately he didn't seem to be aware of how nervous she was or the slight tremor in her hands. They sat together on her small balcony, the Minster tower floodlit and shedding its shadows as the sky, a mixture of purple and scarlet washes, darkened behind the tall structure. They sat in silence for a while, the beautiful evening absorbing their thoughts, until Nick finally spoke.

'I hate to say it,' he said softly, 'but this is like old times.'

Erin had been thinking the same. Fifteen months ago they had sat in this same spot, talking easily about their lives together and unaware of what the future held. Erin nodded slowly, her green eyes coming up to meet Nick's. 'A lot has happened in that time,' she agreed with a catch in her voice.

He looked at her for a long while before he spoke, then, taking a sip of his drink, he said levelly, 'You know, Sherry and I had reached a stalemate in our relationship a long time

94

before I left for England.' He turned his gaze full on her, adding, 'Do you still think of Simon?'

She'd known that he was going to ask her that and she nodded. 'I think of him, but not in the same way as I used to.'

'I suppose what I mean is—are you over him?' Nick raised his eyes to meet hers.

'That's not as easy to answer,' she said quietly. 'I know that he wasn't the person I thought he was and that was the shocking thing. It's taken me a long time to understand that it was me who was at fault, trying to change Simon.'

'Don't we all do that at some point in our relationships, though?'

'Maybe we do. Did it happen with you and Sherry?'

He paused and after a while he shrugged lightly. 'I wanted more out of our relationship than she did—commitment, family life and a future together. Either Sherry didn't want that or she wanted it with someone else. I'm inclined to think it was the latter because last week I heard from a mutual friend that she's now engaged.' He laughed, his tone self-mocking. 'I can only deduce that Sherry wasn't exactly devastated over our split. All in all, I'm quite sure we did the right thing—it would never have worked. It just took me rather a long time to see it, that's all.'

Erin looked at him and wondered what his

reaction had been when he'd received word of Sherry's engagement, and she tried to think back to recall if she had noticed any change in his character. Suddenly it came to her that it could well have been around the time she had been standing in his flat, staring at that photograph of Sherry half-unpacked on the floor.

As she gazed at him she felt the unpleasant tightness in her stomach and she leaned forward to pick up her drink. Had he abandoned the unpacking in dismay? Had he been too upset to carry on? Swallowing the cool liquid, she knew that it was completely irrational that she should feel like this. Perhaps Nick's presence was reminding her again of the past and this was just one of those times when it hurt more than usual to recall.

But as she looked up into his eyes again she knew that her feelings were confused, and some part of her wanted nothing more than to be possessed by the strong arms that lay casually on the table in front of her, his large hands encompassing the glass which was now empty. Is that why she had asked him up here to her flat? Why she had agreed to go to the Lady Jayne with him, using the sketches as a pretext to herself?

Before she realised what was happening, he stood up and moved towards her. He stood above her, and she knew that if he took her into his arms she would not resist.

The sensation that flowed through her was overpowering. Her body ached to be close to him, her skin was flushed with excitement. Every single cell in her body seemed to be aware of his closeness.

Bitter disappointment filled her as he spoke, his voice abrupt. 'I should go,' he muttered. 'It's getting late. Thank you for the drink—and the company. It was a lovely evening.'

Erin watched him walk away, all her instincts being to call out and ask him to stay. But something held her back and, much as she yearned for him, a small voice inside her told her that she would be hurt again and that Sherry was still clearly in his heart and thoughts. He had kissed her—Erin—in the hope he might drive Sherry's memory away, but it was clear now that he hadn't succeeded.

*　　　*　　　*

On the following Friday Erin saw that Tom Knight's name was down for a visit and during her lunch-hour she called on the couple, hoping there had been no further accidents since the last fall. Erin had asked the district nursing team to add Tom and Gladys to their list and she wasn't as concerned as she would have been had there been no supervision for the past couple of weeks.

But when she arrived at the block of flats and the warden let her in, Erin was dismayed to be told that Tom was trapped in the lift and that Gladys was in a severe state of shock.

'The men are up there, repairing the lift,' the warden told Erin, 'and Tom is talking to them through the intercom. He's taking it all in his stride and seems to think it a bit of a joke, but Gladys is almost hysterical.'

'Where is she?' Erin asked, and was told that she had been taken to the lounge where some of the other residents were making her tea. When Erin saw Gladys she knew at once that the concern of the others, well meant as it was, was only upsetting her more.

By the time Erin managed to return the elderly lady to her own flat by way of the working lift, Gladys was shaking uncontrollably and breathing rapidly.

'I c-can't breathe,' Gladys stammered as Erin helped her towards an armchair. 'I—I'm suffocating.'

Erin lowered her gently, taking her hands and squeezing them. 'Gladys, you're hyperventilating through anxiety. I'm going to ask you to breathe into this paper bag, taking slow breaths. I'll explain why as you do it. Do as I say and you'll soon feel better.'

Gladys's eyes were wide as Erin took a paper bag that lay on the table beside them and folded the top around her fingers. Putting it to Gladys's mouth, she encouraged the older woman to breathe into it.

For a moment Gladys still looked scared,

then Erin explained the technique that helped to replace the loss of carbon dioxide from the blood, her voice calm as she watched Gladys slowly respond to the simple remedy. Ten minutes later the crisis was over and, head back against a cushion propped on the chair, Gladys had recovered.

At this point Tom entered the room with the warden, a smile on his face when he saw his wife.

'Tom!' Gladys exclaimed. 'Where have you been?'

'In the garden,' Tom said cheerfully. 'Now I'll make a nice cup of tea for us. Karen, would you like one?'

Erin smiled and shook her head. 'No, thank you, Mr Knight, I'll be on my way soon.'

'He thinks you are our niece,' Gladys sighed. 'He's even forgotten he's been stuck in the lift. The confusion is getting worse. I'm afraid I don't seem to be able to stop getting agitated myself.'

'That's because you are the carer,' Erin said gently, 'and it's very wearing to have to think for the two of you. How are you coping?'

'The nurses are a wonderful help,' Gladys said faintly, 'but the nights are the worst. He's restless and very depressed. Sometimes he's quite aggressive. It's a complete change in character.'

'Would you like Tom to go to a day centre or get some other help from Social Services?'

Erin asked, but even before she'd finished speaking Gladys was shaking her head.

'We've always managed in fifty years of marriage and I'll go on looking after him while I'm able, Dr Brooks.'

'Well, I'll prescribe an antidepressant for Tom, one to be taken each night. That should help him a little and maybe you can both get some rest. Then I think you need something to help settle those nerves of yours.'

'You mean a tranquilliser?' Gladys frowned, then added wearily, 'I never thought it would come to this . . . I really didn't.'

Erin smiled gently. 'Think of it as a temporary help, Mrs Knight. We all need that sometimes, even the fittest—' Erin was stopped by the crash of china. Turning, she saw Tom standing with a broken mug in his hand.

'Here we go,' sighed Gladys as she got up to help her husband.

On the way back to the surgery Erin recalled the bewildered expression on Tom's face and felt a fresh stab of dismay for the sufferers of the cruel dementia that was so debilitating for both sufferer and carer. As she turned into the drive of the surgery, her heart gave an even greater start as her thoughts were catapulted from the Knights to a figure that was climbing into a large red car.

She parked as the car reversed, and stared after it. Blinking again, she strained to identify the driver as the vehicle turned to the left.

With a sensation of disbelief she blinked once more. She was certain she had recognised him, but it couldn't possibly be him—or could it? Was the man she thought she had seen in the car really Simon Forester or had it just been a cruel trick of her imagination?

CHAPTER SIX

Erin paused at Reception and asked Ruth Mathews if anyone had asked for her. But Ruth said that she had only just taken over from the morning staff and that other than her patient, Esme Kelly, waiting to see her, there had been no enquiries.

Erin went to her room and glanced from her window, but there was no sign of the red car or its driver. The more she thought about it, the more illogical it was that Simon would call at the surgery. A year had passed since she had seen him, though she had spoken to him on the telephone just after the cottage had been sold.

Erin walked back to her desk, her thoughts returning to her wedding day. The vicar and her sister forced to announce to the congregation assembled in the Minster that the wedding service had been cancelled. The reception afterwards, at which her mother and father and two sisters had apologised to the guests, encouraging them to eat the delicious food despite the sad event that had taken place. The kindness of Alissa and Max, supporting her when she'd returned to work, her sadness compounded by the sale of the cottage she and Simon had planned to renovate.

Simon had never fully explained his reasons for abandoning her in such a way. She could have understood a gradual deterioration in their relationship and accepted his decision to separate, but she would never understand his cruel rejection, made on their wedding day in front of friends and family.

Lost in thought, Erin looked up to see Ruth standing before her with a mug of coffee. 'Esme and Orion Kelly are just going in to see the nurse,' Ruth said. 'They should only be a few minutes, but it will give you time to have your drink.' She looked at Erin with a frown. 'Are you all right, Dr Brooks?'

Erin nodded, smiling quickly. 'Yes, Ruth, I'm fine. It was just a bit of a rush this morning, that's all.'

'Well, drink that slowly and take your time. Fortunately the mothers and toddlers clinic isn't overflowing. Other than any emergencies, we should have a straightforward afternoon. And before I forget, Dr Darvill said there's to be a final practice run for young Jake on Saturday evening at the Minster. He said it will only take about half an hour and could you fit it in?'

Erin nodded. 'Yes, no problem, Ruth. Tell him I'll be there.'

'OK. I'll leave you to it, then.' Ruth smiled and, leaving Erin to drink her coffee, hurried back to Reception.

Ten minutes later Erin welcomed Esme Kelly and her small son, Orion. 'How is the toilet training coming along?' she asked, and was pleased to hear that young Orion was now doing well during the day.

'You were right, Dr Brooks,' Esme said as she sat with Orion on her knee. 'I was getting too agitated about the whole thing. Orion's doing much better since I haven't put any pressure on him—or on myself.'

'That's good,' Erin said encouragingly as Orion grinned under his curly black hair. At that point Erin realised how much like his father, Sky, the youngster was. She had met Sky several times during their first few months in Hayford Minster, and he was a tall, striking young man who had been uncompromising in his attitude towards traditional medicine. Sky had not been willing to accept Esme's decision to allow Orion to have an operation and that had been when the couple had broken up. Now Esme looked very much her own person. In jeans and sneakers, her hair cut short, she seemed to be asserting her own identity.

'I've had the offer of working at the new

art centre,' Esme said, breaking into Erin's thoughts. 'The trouble is, it would mean I would have to put Orion into nursery full time. It's an opportunity I can't really afford to miss. Financially it would mean that I could come off the benefit system and that really means a lot to me.'

Erin nodded slowly. 'It sounds like a good offer, Esme. Are you going to take it?'

The young woman hesitated. 'I would, but I feel terrible about leaving Orion.'

'Is there a place available for him at nursery?'

'Yes. He could continue in the same one, there's no problem there.'

'He enjoys it?' Erin asked.

'Oh yes, he loves the company.'

'That's reassuring.' Erin smiled. 'You've come a long way in a year, Esme. You should be very proud of yourself and of Orion.'

'It's not been easy, I'll admit,' Esme said quietly. 'And we both still miss Sky.'

'Have you heard from him at all?'

Esme shook her head. 'But my mother wrote to me to say they are coming to see us. It's the first time I've heard from her since I was pregnant with Orion. They've never seen their grandson. I'm feeling a bit nervous about it, especially as I only live in a small studio flat.'

'I'm sure they won't mind and will take everything in their stride. Now, is there

104

anything I can help you with this afternoon?'

Esme nodded and asked Erin to examine Orion, concerned that his small testis had not completely recovered after his operation last year to enable it to descend. Though he had begun to pass urine less frequently, he still complained occasionally of a tummyache. Erin examined him and, after questioning Esme further and finding no obvious problem, decided that she would ask the consultant who had performed surgery on the little boy to see him again.

'Just to be on the safe side,' she told Esme, who explained that her decision to take the new job would rest on the consultant's opinion of Orion's health.

As the two left her room, the child looked back and smiled, his curly black hair shielding a pair of large, bright eyes. Erin returned his smile, and as she sat back in her chair she could not help but have a moment's envy of Esme. As Nick had commented when he'd first seen them, Orion was a striking little boy. With a start, Erin realised that the sensation she was feeling was that of her own unfulfilled motherhood which had clamoured so desperately for recognition and which she had had to suppress as her dreams had been shattered.

*   *   *

105

The Minster was bathed in a soft light and Alissa Darvill watched the two figures walk down the aisle towards them, thinking not for the first time how good they looked together.

Erin was dressed in a long orange skirt and paler blouse, the perfect combination against her tawny skin and glossy brown hair. Her slender figure moved gracefully beside that of Nick's tall one, and Alissa reflected on the long friendship she and Nick had enjoyed, despite her traumatic marriage to Nick's half-brother, Mike.

Sometimes she felt as though she could see an expression in his dark eyes that reminded her of Mike, but it was only fleeting, and with his dark hair and even darker brown eyes he was the opposite in looks to Mike's smaller physique.

Alissa felt a warm wave of pleasure flow over her as Max, sitting close beside her with their son on his lap, moved against her. Beside Max were Bas and Sasha, the two children from their first marriages, and Alissa felt another glow of pride as she looked at them, knowing that these two had a special relationship between them. For that, Alissa would be always grateful, added to which Aaron, Max's eldest son, was responding well to the newly formed family circle.

It was here in this beautiful old building that she and Max had married at Christmas, here that her life had begun with a spiritual blessing that had incorporated the child in her womb and who would be baptised in a week's time.

As Erin approached, with Nick following closely behind, she wished with all her heart that the younger woman would have the good fortune to experience the same depth of love that she herself had found with Max. And if she knew Nick as she thought she did, Erin could be in no better company than that of the man who had been a supportive friend over the years.

With a brief thought to the future, Alissa knew that Erin was determined to leave Hayford Minster and memories of Simon Forester behind her. But would this lead to happiness? Alissa wondered. There had been a time when she, too, had tried to escape the past by leaving Kent and moving to Hayford Minster. But the outcome had resulted in tragedy as her first husband had continued his affair, unwilling to separate from his mistress. A car accident had ended his life as he'd returned from seeing her and it had been then that Alissa had leaned on Nick for support.

Alissa smiled warmly at the two people for whom she cared so deeply. She could wish for no better godparents for Jake than Erin and Nick, and as she kissed Erin lightly on the cheek she hoped that her friend would think seriously about her future before committing herself to leaving the practice.

She glanced briefly towards the back of the

church as a stranger entered but took little notice as the figure stood in the shadows. She was absorbed in watching Erin as she stooped to lift Jake into her arms, an expression on her friend's face that left Alissa in no doubt that the younger doctor was delighted to take possession of her charge as she hugged Jake gently against her.

*   *   *

It was the last week of August and Alec was helping out at the surgery, the pre-term coughs and colds beginning with an outbreak of flu that had the nursing staff busy with arranging flu jabs for the most vulnerable.

Erin hoped that Alec wouldn't be put under too much pressure and was relieved he had decided to take Max and Alissa into his confidence regarding his recent bouts of angina pectoris. The ECG he had undergone, accompanied by tests at the hospital, had resulted in him beginning a regime of medication to increase the blood flow through the heart muscle. This, combined with antihypertensive drugs to reduce the workload of his heart in pumping blood, seemed to have resolved the immediate problem, but Erin was still concerned at his inability to relax.

As Nick joined her on Wednesday morning in the staffroom, Alec was hurtling past them towards the secretary's office. When he saw them he slowed down automatically and Nick stopped him, asking him how he was.

'Absolutely A1 now,' replied Alec briskly. 'Just going to see Jane and get her to write me a few letters on that contraption of hers—one or two referrals that I've had this week. They would take me a month of Sundays to produce but, no doubt, Jane will get them done in a few minutes.' He grinned. 'Then if I can slip away early tonight I shall be taking Aggie out for a spin.'

Erin knew that Alec had problems with the computer system and was out of touch with the newer software that had recently been installed. She was also aware that Alec was still trying to hurry through his day in order to get to his beloved boat, which was moored on the river but due for dry dock in autumn.

Nick shot her a glance as Alec hurried off to find Jane Barr, and as they poured coffee before their surgeries he said quietly, 'Have the attacks got any more frequent, do you know?'

Erin shook her head, pausing to sip her coffee. 'Not that Alec has mentioned.'

'I've a feeling he wouldn't,' Nick responded dully.

'Brian Mateland has arranged an angioplasty,' explained Erin, having read that morning a letter from the cardiologist at the hospital. 'With Alec's family history I don't think there can be any doubt he's at risk.

Alissa said that she met Alec's wife the other day and that nothing was mentioned. She wondered if Alec had said anything to her.'

'Knowing Alec, the answer is probably in the negative,' Nick commented. 'Still, it's reassuring to know Brian Mateland has his case in hand. I just hope Alec slows down a bit while he's here.'

Erin was thoughtful as she drank her coffee. She looked up to see Nick watching her. 'Is there any news on the Fords?' she asked.

'It's over a fortnight since she was admitted,' Nick told her. 'Her husband hasn't been in touch. I can only assume that he still doesn't know about the pregnancy.'

'I had a letter from the hospital, saying that she had been discharged,' Erin said slowly. 'The surgery involved removing the damaged Fallopian tube.'

Nick considered this then shrugged. 'Well, let's hope it all sorts itself out.' He smiled, his dark eyes going over her face, and she felt the colour rush to her cheeks. 'I heard from Fergus, by the way. Unfortunately the portrait won't be ready for the christening this Sunday. Shall we tell Max and Alissa that our gift will be a little late in arriving and leave it at that?'

Erin smiled. 'I hope they won't object to a hint of mystery.'

'A spot of intrigue won't hurt,' Nick assured her with a grin. As they finished their coffee and walked to the door, he added in a curious tone, 'Talking of which, I forgot to mention it but I saw someone looking into your car the other day as I left for my visits. As I approached he hurried off even though I called out, asking if I could help him.'

'Can you describe him?' Erin asked.

'Fairish, close-cropped hair, well dressed, mid-thirties. City type, not your usual green-wellie rustic. Jumped into a red Ford and drove off like a bat out of hell.'

With a sinking sensation in her stomach, Erin was silent, her heart beginning to beat rapidly, aware that the description Nick had just given her fitted Simon perfectly.

*   *   *

It was Sunday and Erin stood beside Nick, entranced by the scene before her.

'I baptise thee . . . Jake Sebastien Darvill . . .' The beautiful words echoed into the timbers of the Minster and there was silence as the christening group looked at the eleven-month-old baby who giggled as the vicar dropped holy water on his forehead.

'Not a whisper from him,' whispered Erin as she leaned toward Nick.

'He's a great little chap,' Nick said in a soft voice, his warm breath fanning Erin's ear. 'If only they could be made to order.'

She laughed softly, glancing up into Nick's eyes, and for a moment he held her gaze, the moment seeming to go on for a long time as the world revolved about them. But soon they were brought back to reality, both stepping forward towards the font and the plump, happy child in the vicar's arms.

When the poignant service was over, Nick and Erin were the first to leave the chapel. Nick slid his hand around Erin's waist as they walked towards the great oak doors. 'We're invited back for the christening party. Will you come in my car?'

She looked up at him and nodded. 'Yes . . . why not?'

Again he held her gaze and it was then she realised that something had changed between them, a subtle altering of their relationship that she could not give a name to. Whatever it was, she couldn't deny it and as they stood, waiting for their godson and his parents, brothers and sister to emerge from the chapel, Nick folded his fingers around hers. 'September,' he whispered softly as a breeze blew in the scent of falling leaves and bonfires. 'A beautiful month.'

She nodded, thinking that she felt happy. Truly happy. She couldn't analyse the feeling, she was almost afraid to admit it, but she knew this was a day that she would always remember. As the family behind them broke into soft chatter, she moved with Nick to the open doors and gazed out onto the green grass of the Minster lawn and the gravel pathway leading down to the lych gate towards which the children were already running.

It was a perfect pastoral scene and one that Erin had always dreamed of as a little girl—the church, the village, the rural setting that she had always yearned to be a part of. A community much like her own in Ireland where she had been born. The countryside was in her blood, the green fields and swathes of autumn woods. When she had trained in London, her unswerving aim had been to return to the setting that had given her so much pleasure as a child and her dream had almost been fulfilled. Almost . . .

As Nick walked with her to the gate, she felt his fingers tighten around hers. This was the path she had walked up in her bridal gown, and as she looked up at him she wondered what it would have been like to have walked down the aisle to meet the man who was now by her side.

Her face was thoughtful as Nick stared down at her, his dark eyes taking in the loveliness of the young woman whose hand was clasped firmly in his own. Then, with a suddenness that startled Erin, a figure appeared before them as Nick pushed open the gate.

'Hello, Erin,' the stranger said. And Erin looked up into the pale blue eyes of the man she had once planned to marry.

It took several moments for Erin to recover

113

from the shock as Simon stood there in a grey suit and tie, staring down at her. Erin glanced at Nick who hadn't moved and was studying the other man intently as the three of them stood by the gate. Attempting to gather herself, she said briskly, 'What is it you want, Simon?'

The fair-haired man hesitated. 'Just a few words with you, Erin, that's all. I realise I may have called at a difficult time, but I'm only in Hayford Minster for a few hours.'

'We've nothing to say to one another, Simon,' she answered, trying not to allow her voice to shake.

Simon said quickly, 'It's about the sale of the cottage. Perhaps you've noticed that no one has moved in yet?'

Erin shook her head. 'No, I haven't been past it.'

'Well, it's empty and . . .' Simon glanced at Nick and, shrugging, said shortly, 'This is rather complicated. I do really need to talk to you.'

Erin was thrown into confusion and, sensing Nick's presence beside her, she felt a distinct air of hostility between the two men. She had no wish to see Simon alone and since their last discussion on the phone, which had ended coldly, she hadn't heard from him in almost a year.

'Look, I'll wait for you in my car over there.' He gestured to the red Ford parked on the opposite side of the road. 'As I said, it won't take too long. Perhaps we could go somewhere for a drink, and once I've explained this matter to you I'll be on way.'

'I'm about to meet friends.' Erin paused, then thought that perhaps she was evading the inevitable and would rather get it over with now that he was here. 'But as long as I'm quick,' she added hastily. 'You'd better come back to the flat.'

Simon nodded and turned, giving Nick a cursory glance. As he climbed into the car Nick looked down at Erin, frowning. 'It's none of my business, but do you think you're doing the right thing, seeing him alone?'

Erin looked up into Nick's face, recalling that only moments ago her hand had been curled in his, and that she had felt the closeness between them as they'd stood together in the Minster. Now she could feel his antagonism towards Simon and she was in a difficult position.

'He said it was to do with the cottage,' she said hesitantly. 'And if the place is still unoccupied, then I would like to know what has happened.'

'Shouldn't your solicitor be dealing with this kind of problem?' Nick frowned.

'Yes, possibly. And should there be a complication—though I can't think what—I'll refer Simon to him.'

It was Alissa who spoke next as she came

up to join them. 'Erin, was that who I think it was?' she asked, the surprise evident in her voice.

Erin nodded, her cheeks flushed. 'Yes. I'm as surprised as you are.'

'He was the person I saw looking in your car the other day,' Nick said tautly. 'Obviously he's been trying to see you.'

Max approached with Jake in his arms and, standing beside his wife, he glanced at the red Ford, then at Erin. 'Is there trouble, Erin?'

She shook her head. 'No, I don't think so. Simon said that the cottage is unoccupied still and that he would like to talk about it.'

'Are you going to do as he asks?' Max frowned.

'Yes,' Erin said quickly, realising her friends were concerned for her. 'I shall only be a short while—I would prefer to get this conversation over and done with rather than postpone it.'

Alissa nodded, and as Bas and Sasha ran towards them she said, glancing at Nick, 'You'll join us at the house, then?'

'We've got a lovely party ready, Aunt Erin,' called Sasha, her brown ponytail swinging as she stood beside Max. 'You won't be late, will you?' asked Alissa's eight-year-old daughter, oblivious of the tension in the air.

'No, I shan't,' Erin said, and bent to give her a hug, saying a brief goodbye as the family moved off to Max's Land Rover. Nick was still staring at Erin, his brows drawn together in a

116

deep crease.

'I have to say I don't like the idea of you going on your own,' Nick told her in a low voice. 'Would you care for some company?'

'No, thanks all the same,' she said, and smiled. 'I'll see you soon.'

Nick lifted his shoulders in a shrug then glanced over to the car where Simon Forester was sitting, watching them. 'I hope you know what you're doing, Erin,' he added darkly.

*   *   *

'The Oxtons' business has collapsed and they may soon be forced into receivership,' Simon explained as, back at the flat, Erin handed him a coffee as he sat on the sofa. 'They want to sell the cottage and realise what collateral they can.'

She took a cup from the tray and walked to the chair by the window to sit down opposite him. He had undone the buttons of his grey suit jacket and was leaning forward as he sat on the sofa, his elbows on his knees, his fair head bent as he talked to her and stirred his coffee.

She knew him so well, knew his body language and the way he had of speaking. At one time she had been attracted to that, to his casual charm and the pretence of interest he had displayed, but now, with sudden distaste, she wanted nothing more than to end this conversation. She moved to the edge of her seat, hoping that he would come to the point swiftly.

'Paul Oxton rang me last month and made this proposal,' Simon said as he looked up at her. 'I came to see you before, but unfortunately I must have missed you. I'm afraid I was a bit short on time,' he said, shrugging. 'And I knew you would probably be busy anyway.'

'What has this to do with me?' Erin asked as she recalled the ridiculously low price they had accepted for the cottage, a price which had been agreed on by all parties because of the circumstances. Erin had wanted nothing more than to be rid of unhappy memories and Simon had been as eager as she to put the sale behind him. As for the Oxtons, a middle-aged couple who ran a haulage business, they were only too pleased to snap up what had definitely been a bargain.

'It has everything to do with you—with us,' Simon said, and her heart gave a leap at his last words. 'They have offered the place back to us at the same price.'

'But why?' Erin asked doubtfully. 'They could sell it for far more than they gave, even in its present condition.'

Simon gave her a tight smile. 'Their business is failing and they want to liquidate their assets swiftly. If we were to buy it back, have it renovated and sell next year, it would be a sound business investment. The last time we spoke on the telephone—'

'Over a year ago,' Erin reminded him swiftly.

'Was it?' He looked at her blankly. 'Well, yes, all right, then—but at that time you said you were looking for somewhere else other than the apartment—'

'I hadn't made my mind up what I wanted to do,' Erin broke in once more, unable to understand where the conversation was leading. 'I was still in a state of shock—or perhaps you weren't aware of that?'

He looked at her sheepishly. 'I tried to explain that I didn't mean to hurt you,' he protested. 'Look, Erin, I know I hurt you badly but this proposition from the Oxtons could be a turning point for us. I behaved unforgivably and I want to make it up to you. What better way for us than having back the cottage?'

Erin shook her head slowly, her full mouth falling open. 'Simon, I want nothing more to do with the cottage, or with you. I can't believe that you think I would be the slightest bit interested in the Oxtons' proposal. If you want the cottage, I suggest you buy it, but don't involve me.'

At this he put his cup down and raised his eyes to hers. 'Erin, don't you see what I'm trying to do?'

She looked at him and saw the narrowness of his features, the blue eyes that no longer held any allure and the selfish mouth that was turned up into a pleading smile. 'Erin, I'm trying to say sorry . . . and if you will accept my apology, I want us to try again.'

Erin's green eyes grew wide in disbelief. 'Do you seriously believe that we could ever build a relationship together,' she said hoarsely, 'after what has happened? Simon, you walked out on me on our wedding day. You left me to pick up the pieces of my life and you didn't ever give me a satisfactory explanation. And now you're asking to pick up where we left off?'

'Why not?' he asked as he rose and walked towards her. 'I was badly misled before. I made a mistake and I'm trying to rectify it.'

'How were you misled?' Erin looked up at him, her expression bewildered.

'By someone else,' he said, pausing as though deciding how much to tell her. 'Someone who at the time caused me to believe that my future did not lie here in Hayford Minster.'

Erin stood up slowly, realising that after all this time the truth was finally emerging. She waited, breath held, as Simon ran his hands through his hair and, finally giving his head a little shake, sighed. 'If you must know, I got involved with a colleague at work. It was just a brief fling and was over in a few weeks. She meant nothing to me, but at the time I felt that I just couldn't go through with our plans. I was confused and misled—but now I see how foolishly I behaved.'

Erin swallowed, her hands clenched at her sides. 'Are you telling me there was someone else?' she asked weakly.

Simon looked at her, his face full of self-pity, and she listened as the excuses began, his hands reaching out to draw her towards him. Involuntarily she recoiled, aware that she had never known this man at all.

CHAPTER SEVEN

Erin could not remember clearly what happened next, only that she pulled herself free, walked towards the door and opened it, her voice unnaturally calm as she asked Simon to leave.

Now she stared down at the figure walking towards the vehicle parked in the lane beneath her window. He had stalked out of her flat like a child in a tantrum and she asked herself how it was possible that she had ever loved this man. How could she have considered making her life with him?

The rest of their brief conversation echoed through her brain as she saw him unlock the sports car and climb into it without even glancing up at her window. For a moment she admitted a satisfaction at the humiliation that had been etched on his face, a look of incredulity at her insistence that he leave the flat and that she wanted nothing more to do with him. As the car moved off, she gave way to the emotion that filled her, a sense of relief and sadness mixing within her at the thought that she might now have been living in an unhappy marriage with a man who had obviously thought very little of her.

As she turned away from the window the telephone rang, and she brushed the moistness from her eyes, going over to pick it up and clearing her throat before she spoke.

The voice was deep and concerned, and a wave of warmth went through her at the sound of it. 'Erin, are you all right?' Nick asked.

She sat down on the sofa, her hands shaking a little. 'Yes, I'm fine. I was just about to drive over.'

'Would you like me to come and collect you?'

'No, I shan't be long.'

There was a brief pause before he said, 'The children are asking for you.'

'Oh, are they?' Erin immediately stood up, brushing down the pale pink skirt of her suit. 'I . . . I'm leaving right away.'

'Drive carefully, then,' he told her, and as Erin put down the telephone she recalled the brief moment before Simon had left when he'd demanded to know if she was seeing the man with whom she had been walking earlier. She had opened the door and looked at him with

122

pity, an expression which must have hurt him as his face had grown dark and he had left, her answer unnecessary as he had thundered down the stairs.

*   *   *

The new house that the Darvills had moved into in February was filled with laughter and music as the occasion gave them an opportunity to celebrate.

Alissa spoke to Erin briefly as she helped replenish the buffet in the large kitchen, but Erin kept her comments simple, saying that Simon had called about the cottage, omitting to go into detail about his other remarks.

But with Nick it was a different situation and several times throughout the afternoon he met her gaze questioningly. She told him the same as she had told Alissa and yet she knew that he suspected more.

He didn't presume to enquire further, though, and it wasn't until Erin decided it was time to leave, and slid on the jacket of her pink suit, that he spoke to her next.

'Are you leaving?' he asked her as she looked up to find that the hall wasn't deserted and that he had been standing there, watching her.

'Yes, I would stay and help clear away the debris, but Alissa won't have it. She's insistent that she and Max and the children can manage after everyone has gone.'

'Have you said goodbye?' he asked, hesitating.

'No, I thought I would now. I can hear the children playing in the garden. I thought I would go to see them first.'

'Do you mind if I come with you?'

She smoothed down the silky material of her jacket and did up the one button at her waist. 'Not at all, Nick. Are you leaving too?'

He raised his eyes to hers. 'I'd like some time to spend with you. Or did you have other plans?'

It was a comment that caught her off guard and yet touched her, though she was beginning to feel as if all she wanted to do was lie in a bath and allow the thoughts that had been gathering on the edge of her mind all day to flow freely around her head. She knew that this could only be attempted in silence and comfort, but she also realised that Nick was staring at her with some concern and that she owed him more of an explanation than she had given him regarding Simon's visit.

'Thank you both so much for making this a special day,' Alissa said as she and Max walked with them to the cars parked in the drive. The elegant house that stood behind them was beginning to quieten down after the party, and Aaron's bedroom window was open, the pounding beat of a popular group moderated to a level acceptable to adults.

Alissa touched Erin's arm. 'Is everything really all right?' she asked softly. 'We haven't had much chance to talk. There was no trouble with Simon, was there?'

Erin looked at her friend and smiled. 'Not now, no. But I have to say that you warned me about Simon's motivation for opting out of our wedding and it appears you were right.'

'You mean there was someone else?'

'Yes.' Erin raised her eyebrows and sighed. 'It was just a fling apparently, according to Simon.'

'A fling that almost wrecked your life,' Alissa commented. 'I'm sorry, Erin, but it's evident that Simon did you a favour that day, even though it may not have seemed like it at the time.'

'I know that now.' Alissa touched her friend's hand. 'Go back and enjoy the rest of your party.'

'Nick was concerned about you,' Alissa said as she paused, before leaving. 'He really didn't seem to be able to settle while you were away. And when Sherry telephoned I noticed that he was very brief with her.'

'Sherry phoned him here?' Erin asked in surprise.

Alissa shook her head. 'As I say, Nick wasn't in the least bit interested and, though he didn't comment on what she wanted, I had the distinct impression that his mind wasn't on their conversation.'

Erin tried to keep the disappointment from her face. She knew she was being irrational in feeling the way she did. But what had Sherry wanted? And how had she known that Nick was at Alissa's? Had he given her the number and explained where he would be during the afternoon? In which case, they were still on close terms.

Erin decided that the exhaustion of the day was suddenly catching up with her. Taking care not to let her feelings show, she said her goodbyes and drove away, operating the car automatically as her thoughts once again were in turmoil.

Her eyes suddenly felt heavy and the weariness that had threatened earlier, after she had spoken to Simon, now seemed to be taking hold of her limbs and draining her. She realised that shock was the cause and that to recover she needed time by herself.

However, she was aware of Nick's car as he followed her at a distance, and she knew that, shattered as she felt, she had to speak to him before she was able to grasp the peace she so desperately needed.

'My flat or yours?' Nick asked as he walked across the lane towards her. Erin finished locking her car, turning to face him.

'Can this wait until tomorrow, Nick?' she asked in what she hoped sounded like a reasonable tone.

'I know you must be tired,' he answered with

a confused frown, 'but we've barely spoken all afternoon. Earlier today, in the Minster, I had hoped that we had . . .' He stopped, lifting his dark eyes to hers. 'Well, I thought—mistakenly, it seems—that at last the barriers that seemed to have been erected between us since last year had come down. Then Simon Forester appeared and your attitude changed again when I saw you next.'

'My attitude has nothing to do with Simon,' she protested, finding herself at once on the defensive, then added as she realised how abrupt she sounded, 'I know that you were concerned for me, and I don't want to appear ungrateful. I'll come in with you for a few minutes.'

He hesitated, his brow creasing into a frown, then he turned and walked towards his door, reaching down into his trouser pocket for his key.

Inside the flat, all was all tidy now, and to Erin's surprise there were no photographs on display. Two large modern art prints were now positioned on the walls, and the shelves of the bookcases were lined with books.

'What would you like to drink?' Nick asked.

Erin hesitated as she decided where to sit. Walking to one of the large leather chairs, she said, 'Something cold, I think—orange juice would be lovely.'

Nick nodded, removing the jacket of his dark suit as he walked towards the kitchen.

He wore a crisp white shirt and his shoulders moved under the material with an easy motion, his dark hair brushing the collar as he thrust the coat onto the back of a chair.

Minutes later he returned with two drinks in tall glasses, placing one beside her on the coffee-table. She took a sip and leaned back, her head resting on the cool leather. He sat opposite her, the tension between them evident. She watched him sink into the comfortable leather of the sofa and, stretching a long arm across the back of it, loosen his tie. For several moments they said nothing and then as he looked across at her, she spoke.

'It seems that Simon was contacted by the people who bought the cottage from us. They asked if we would like to buy it back again as they have fallen on hard times.'

'Why should they think you would be interested?' Nick asked, frowning.

'I've no idea,' she answered with a shrug. 'I think they were clutching at straws because of their circumstances and trying all avenues.'

'Are you interested in the proposal?' Nick's frown deepened.

'No, not at all. I've made my plans for next year and I see no reason to change them. If I decide to rent or buy somewhere else it certainly won't be in Hayford Minster.'

'You've decided to accept the job at the private health clinic?' he asked in a low voice.

Taking a deep breath, she stood up. 'Nick

. . . I really don't feel like discussing this now. I admit it was a shock, seeing Simon, and it must have shown on my face and, of course, I'm grateful for your concern—for everyone's concern . . . but—'

'But you would rather I didn't interfere,' he interrupted her, standing up, too. 'Is that what you're saying? Erin, can't you see that I don't want to intrude in your life? I thought we shared something special between us . . . an attraction that I can't ignore and I don't think you can either. I felt close to you earlier today and I thought you felt the same way. Now, if I'm wrong I'll understand and keep my distance. But if I'm right . . .'

Erin felt her heart race as his voice tailed off, his eyes locking with hers, the question in them unavoidable. She couldn't deny that he was right, that in the Minster, as she had felt his presence beside her, she had forgotten everything but the wonder of the moment they had shared together. And had it not been for Simon's arrival she knew that the afternoon would have turned out quite differently to this.

Perhaps because of this thought, she didn't resist as he moved forward and reached down to take her hands and lift her to her feet, bringing her against him in an embrace that made it clear he intended to kiss her.

'Erin, I've waited a long time to hold you in my arms,' he said softly, 'and I make no apology for doing it now.' He reached down to tilt up her chin, his dark gaze intense on her pale face as he looked into her eyes. 'I want you, Erin. You know that, don't you?'

She felt powerless to move and her heart raced erratically in her chest as slowly he lowered his lips to hers. The kiss was shatteringly real and as she closed her eyes and gave herself up to the magic that seemed to be encompassing them, her hands slipped around his neck and she felt the power of his strong body melt against her.

There was little she could do but respond, her body apparently giving up all right to free will as he brought her closer, the kiss deepening as she leaned against him, a thrill of excitement sweeping through her like wildfire. It was a heat that grew stronger as his tongue entered her mouth and searched for a response, challenging her to protest against the sweet pleasure that was filling her.

Moments seemed to slip away as the pressure of his hands against her body increased, her breath coming shallowly as she gave herself up to the onslaught of his kisses. She could feel her heart beating rapidly and her chest rising and falling with excitement, leaving her aching for more. It was as she realised she was losing control that she finally became aware of her surroundings again and, pushing gently against him, she shook her head.

'No . . . Nick . . . no.'

He held her to him. 'Why not, Erin? What are you afraid of?'

'N-nothing, but this isn't the right time.' She bit her lip as she looked up at him, her whole body trembling as she tried to think of the words to say. How could she express how vulnerable she felt, how she needed to protect herself against the repetition of the hurt which had once shattered her life? How could she ever trust again when only this afternoon she had been made aware of how little she had really understood Simon—a man whom she had known for seven years and yet had known so little about.

And what of Nick's former love, Sherry? Hadn't it only been this afternoon that she had tried to get in contact with him? Was it really all over between them, or was this just an interlude in their affair? It was clear that Sherry still meant something to him and possibly always would. Taking a deep breath, she pushed herself away and, taking a moment to compose herself, she walked towards the window and looked out onto the scene before her. There were stars glowing in a misty blue sky above a sunset that would not dissipate as it clung to the last scarlet rays of a September evening. A little while later she felt him beside her, and she was torn between the need to turn and fold her arms around him and a fear that if she did so the result would be inevitable.

'I must have been reading all the wrong

signals,' he said quietly. 'I apologise.'

She turned to say that he was wrong but he suddenly turned and moved to the chair she had been sitting in, picking up her bag.

'Don't forget this,' he said quietly, his eyes now avoiding hers. 'I'll see you out.'

'Nick—' she began, taking the bag with shaking hands, but he was already on his way to the door and her voice faded as the old hinges creaked.

'I'll wait for you to let yourself in,' he said as she fumbled for a key outside her own door. 'Goodnight, Erin.'

There was a moment's hesitation between them, then she forced herself to move and slid her key into her own lock.

As she closed the door she heard his latch go down after he was sure that she had entered safely.

Inside her own flat it was silent and warm, but a few crispy brown leaves had blown in behind her on the breeze. As she ascended the stairs she shivered, folding her arms about her as she did so as though to protect herself from her emotions which felt as confused as the autumn leaves.

*   *   *

The following week brought rain and grey skies. With the change in weather came heavy colds and the spread of the flu that had threatened earlier in the month.

On Monday of that week one of the casualties was Marina Ford and Erin went to visit her on a dark and rainy Thursday, the morning bringing with it a faint hint of winter. As she drove into the drive of the big house, the lights were on and shone out onto the garden. Desmond Ford opened the door to Erin's ring and showed her upstairs to the bedroom in which Erin had last spoken to Pauline.

As she smiled at Marina, tucked up in bed, she listened to Desmond who explained that he'd had to collect his daughter from school earlier in the week and that since then she had not been well. Although she'd only had a light cold, it had now developed and it was obvious that her father was concerned.

'Now, Marina, tell me what's wrong,' Erin said as she sat on the bed.

'I felt sick at school on Monday, then my legs went all funny.' Marina coughed as Erin listened to her chest and the nasty rattle that had developed inside it.

'Marina has a chest infection,' Erin explained after she had made a full examination. 'Is she allergic to penicillin?' Desmond shook his head and Erin wrote out a prescription for the antibiotic. 'A five-day course should do the trick,' she told him, 'but if you are concerned at any point, call in to the surgery right away.'

'Is it the flu, Doctor?' he asked anxiously.

'It may have started that way,' Erin said as she stood up and handed over the prescription, 'but it has left some congestion on her chest.'

After a few words of reassurance with Marina, Erin said goodbye to the little girl and Desmond accompanied her downstairs. As they stood in the hall, Desmond hesitated, before showing her to the door. 'She is going to be all right?' he asked, his face showing the deep lines of anxiety which now seemed more accentuated.

Erin nodded. 'Yes, the antibiotic will start to take effect after a day or two. Keep her warm and rested, and as soon as the infection clears you'll find she'll be back to normal very quickly.'

He nodded, giving way to a long sigh. 'I feel very inadequate,' he said quietly. 'I'm trying to compensate for my wife's absence. I'm afraid we're separated and the more I try, the more I seem to fail. My housekeeper tells me that Marina has been asking for Pauline while I'm at work. Yesterday I decided I would take time off and try to make sure Marina got the attention she feels she's missing out on.' He raised his eyes to Erin. 'It's at times like this I realise how Pauline must have felt. I just left it all to her, assuming that she'd cope. We both wanted so much out of life—a nice home, cars, a good standard of living . . .'

'Perhaps you needed a little more time,'

Erin said sympathetically. 'Time with each other and with Marina.'

Desmond nodded. 'Yes, I can see that now. And I can understand now why she didn't want a bigger family. That was always a bone of contention between us.' He sighed. 'Now that I've had to cope with the home and Marina for the last few months, well, I appreciate how difficult it was for her to hold down a full-time career and take care of the home.'

'Have you discussed this with your wife?' Erin asked.

'You mean, have I told her what I've just told you?' He shook his head. 'No, I'm afraid I've been late in waking up to the fact. I've built my own business up from scratch. The cost of success, it appears, is my family. Pauline and I have forgotten how to communicate other than through third parties—my housekeeper, the school, her solicitor and mine. It's a vicious circle after a while.'

It was then that Erin sensed that even though the marriage was in jeopardy, Desmond at least was aware of his shortcomings, and when Erin returned to the surgery she decided to speak to Nick.

It was late in the afternoon by the time she managed to see him—his surgery had been prolonged by several emergencies and he was about to leave when she knocked on his door.

'Hello, there,' he said, and she thought how

tired he looked, his face strained and his eyes shadowed by dark rings. 'Come in.'

She watched him walk to a cupboard and tidy away a few books and papers, then he turned and reached for his jacket which hung on the back of a chair. Sliding it on, one long arm after the other, he shrugged it into place, finally sinking into his seat and looking at her.

It was the first time they had spoken at length together since the christening. They had passed the minimum of comments on their way in and out of the surgery and had even met outside their front doors on one occasion, but each of them had taken care not to say more than was necessary, both resorting to the topic of the weather, before hurrying off in opposite directions.

Now she wondered if he was feeling well, or if, perhaps, he had fallen prey to the flu which had kept them so busy in surgery. 'I thought that I would just like to tell you that I've seen your little patient, Marina Ford, today. She has a nasty chest infection after the flu, but there's no reason to think she won't recover soon enough.'

Nick frowned. 'What was the domestic situation? I haven't heard from Desmond recently.'

'Still much the same, I should think,' Erin said hesitantly, then outlined what Desmond had told her during her visit. As she was speaking Nick's face lost some of its tiredness,

136

his dark eyes slowly focusing on her. As she concluded, he leaned forward, nodding slowly.

'So you think there may be hope for the marriage yet?' he asked as he looked at her.

'I wish I knew,' Erin said with a shrug. 'But one thing struck me and that was the concern that Desmond showed for his wife, rather than bitterness or resentment.'

'Having to take time off for Marina has caused him to think again, you mean,' Nick suggested.

Erin nodded thoughtfully. 'It's clear both of them were achievers and didn't realise how much they were growing apart. They have a lovely home and everything they've strived for, but they've lost each other along the way. However, Pauline didn't want him to know of the pregnancy, which obviously means she didn't want to upset him. You see, it was Desmond who wanted more children, not Pauline.'

'And a younger man comes on the scene and within six months she's expecting,' Nick guessed. 'Yes, you may have a point.' He took a deep breath, expelling it slowly. 'To change the subject, I called on a couple yesterday evening at about half past ten in the evening. I think you know them, the Knights.'

Erin nodded. 'Yes—not another fall?'

He shook his head. 'No, Gladys had flu, but the problem was Tom. He was very confused when I arrived and it was that which was concerning his wife. He had left the bedroom that morning and she hadn't known where he was going or what he was doing. Fortunately one of the neighbours accompanied him back.'

'I last prescribed an antidepressant,' Erin said, leaning forward. 'Has it helped at all?'

'Gladys hasn't yet had the prescription dispensed. Because of the flu, she's been incapacitated. On the whole, I felt we had to step in and ask Social Services to call, along with a psychiatric nurse to make an assessment of the case. Gladys needs to go in for a hip replacement soon and Tom will need care.'

'Has she heard from the hospital yet?' Erin asked.

'Yes, just that day. They've given her a date for early October.'

'Good.' Erin sighed. 'October certainly won't be before time.'

There was a brief silence before Nick spoke again. 'How is Alec doing?' he asked uncertainly. 'Has he mentioned those tests?'

Erin had spoken to Alec the previous day and he seemed to be taking his health problem seriously, attending the tests that had been arranged at the cardiology department of the hospital. She explained this to Nick who nodded as he listened, but she could see that he was as uneasy as she felt about the further three weeks that Alec was still to undertake as locum.

'With Christmas looming,' Nick said quietly,

'I think we shall have to look for someone to start here earlier than next year. There will be your place to be filled and none of us want to pressure Alec into extra work over the holiday period. Even if we haven't organised a replacement GP, I think we should have a locum in mind. Max and Alissa have suggested that we settle the details the week after your interview—which is, Alissa said, a week tomorrow.'

With a sudden wave of dismay, Erin realised that her final interview for the job in London was not far off. Once she was through that, the probability was that she would be offered the post at the private clinic. As she looked at Nick and felt his eyes on her, she realised that it was now up to her to agree with his comments. Swallowing, she nodded. 'Yes, that's right,' she confirmed as she pulled back her shoulders. 'I should know the exact dates on my return.'

'Well, if I suggest to Kirstie that we set up the meeting for the following Monday, we should be able to settle all the loose ends then.' He cast her a glance and she knew that he was waiting for her to speak.

For some reason she felt totally unprepared for what she knew was inevitable and for what she thought she had come to terms with—a future back in the City in private practice. But something had changed inside her after Simon's visit and now at the mention of the interview she had to try to summon up enthusiasm.

Had Nick been right when he'd accused her of running away? And if he had been, why had she not realised it before? She took a breath and made a concerted effort to compose herself. She was just experiencing a moment's doubt, something that everyone went through before making a change in their lives. Once the interview was over she would feel better about the whole thing—a thought that left her even more devoid of enthusiasm as she looked up into Nick's dark brown eyes and had to steel herself to agree with all he'd just suggested.

CHAPTER EIGHT

It was on the following Monday evening that Erin called at the supermarket in Hayford Minster. Having selected the bread and fresh milk that she needed, she stood at the checkout and happened to notice a couple walking towards the exit. She recognised Mark Longman at once and then her eyes went to the woman beside him, Pauline Ford. They were unaware of her gaze as they stopped before the large glass doors, and for a moment she saw Pauline hesitate while Mark made his way back into the store again.

It was unavoidable that Erin should pass by her and, nearing the exit, Erin smiled, noting that her patient looked away as she approached.

'How are you, Mrs Ford?' Erin asked, noticing that Pauline's hair looked disarranged and fell over her face.

'OK, thanks,' Pauline answered her hesitantly. 'How is Marina? Is she any better? Have you seen her?'

'Yes, I have—but haven't you seen her yourself this weekend?' Erin frowned, recalling that Pauline's arrangement was to have her daughter with her on Saturdays and Sundays.

'No . . . I couldn't go and I know that she's had flu . . .' Erin sensed that she was distressed as she looked down at the floor, hiding her face. Then, as she turned slightly to one side, Erin saw the bruising.

'Have you had an accident?' Erin was shocked at the sight of the discoloration around her patient's eye and cheek.

Pauline shook her head. 'It was nothing. I . . . I fell over, that's all.'

'Shouldn't you have come in to see me?' Erin became slowly aware that Pauline seemed to have lost weight and was very pale.

'There's nothing wrong with me . . . I . . . just wanted to know how Marina—' Pauline stopped abruptly and stepped back. 'I'm afraid I can't talk to you now. I must go.'

At that moment the tall figure of Mark approached, a newspaper in his hand. Casting a brief glance at Erin, he gestured Pauline towards the exit. Erin watched them leave, her suspicions aroused as the tall man gripped his companion's arm tightly and steered her across the road.

Erin stood for a moment, watching them, and as she did so she felt a chill sweep over her. There could be no doubt that the look she had seen in Pauline's eyes was one of fear. And as the full meaning of this became clear to Erin, she knew that she would have to try to help in some way, though how she was to do that she was at a loss to know as Pauline was obviously too frightened to reveal what was happening to her.

*   *   *

The following morning Erin called at the Fords' large house on her way to the surgery and, catching Desmond just before he left for work, saw that Marina was sitting in the back of the car dressed in her school uniform.

'She's much better, thanks,' Desmond said to her enquiry about Marina, though he looked surprised. 'She was a little disappointed her mother couldn't visit at the weekend,' he said rather abruptly, 'but we were told that she had the flu, too, and didn't want to pass it back to Marina.'

Erin nodded, smiling at the little girl. 'Just as well,' she said, though what he had just told her made her even more certain that there was something quite wrong. She wondered who had passed the message on and whether or not it had been Mark, but she didn't want to arouse Desmond's suspicions and left it at that.

After she had said goodbye and returned to surgery, the question of Pauline's welfare still troubled her as she spoke to her first patient, Esme Kelly. But she managed to put it to the back of her mind as the young mother sitting before her explained that she had received good news from the hospital.

'Orion's operation to correct his undescended testis has been completely successful,' Esme told her. 'He's just rather slow with his toilet training, but the consultant said there was nothing wrong otherwise. So I've decided to take the job at the art centre that I was telling you about. It means I'll be able to come off benefits and make a career for myself.'

'I'm very glad to hear it,' Erin said encouragingly. 'When do you start?'

'Next week. My parents, who visited us for the first time this summer, have offered to come and help me with Orion for the first month. The art centre provide day care for the employees' children and Mum and Dad are going to take Orion into the crèche in the mornings and then look after him themselves in the afternoons. If it all goes well, the crèche will find him a full-time place in October.'

Esme paused, looking down at her hands, then said quickly, 'There's just one problem and that is that last night I found a lump in my breast. Just when everything had started going well . . . I couldn't believe it.'

'Let me have a look, then,' Erin said gently. 'Just take your blouse and bra off, and lie on the couch. Do you know if anyone in the family has had breast problems?'

Esme shook her head. 'No. I asked my mother this morning and she said that neither she nor her sister has had any trouble, nor their mother.'

'And this is the first time you've found a lump?'

Esme nodded as she lay on the couch. 'I've got rather tender breasts and before my period it's worse, but I'm just finished and this lump still seems to be there.'

Erin made her examination, raising Esme's arms and pressing under and around her breasts in a clockwise direction, finally arriving at the area on the left breast that was worrying Esme.

'I don't think you've anything to be concerned about,' Erin said as she stepped away and allowed Esme to dress again. 'You may be going through some hormonal changes, causing your breasts to be lumpy, but just to make sure we'll get you in to see Mr Timson, who will, no doubt, send you for a mammogram.'

'You mean a breast X-ray?' Esme said doubtfully. 'But how long will that take?'

'Not long. Outpatients will send you an appointment in the next week or so.' Erin smiled reassuringly as she sat for a few moments more, trying to reassure her young patient.

When Esme left, Erin sighed as she glanced once more over the girl's notes. Esme hadn't had an easy time over the past few years, neither, it appeared, had Pauline Ford, who returned to her thoughts once again. In Esme's case, a swift assessment at the breast clinic would be the first step, followed by a mammogram or a breast scan. But how could she help Pauline Ford? she wondered as she glanced out of the window into the bright September's day.

It was when she saw Nick climb out of his car and stride towards the surgery that she realised she had to discuss it with him as soon as possible, for she was in no doubt now as to the urgency of the matter.

'You're certain the bruising couldn't have been caused by a fall?' Nick frowned as he sat at his desk, turning a pen over between his fingers as he digested all that Erin had just told him.

'I'm not certain, no,' Erin said as she gazed from the window onto the small garden outside, 'but adding one fact to another, I'm very concerned about Pauline. And bearing

145

in mind that her little girl goes to visit her—
and children aren't liked by Mark, by Pauline's
own admission—I would say that the chances
are she's in an unsafe relationship and Marina
is therefore at risk.'

'Those are weighty assumptions to arrive at,'
Nick reminded her, and Erin nodded as she
turned to look at him.

'Yes, they are. But I can't ignore the fact
that I've seen my patient who has been badly
injured, heard from her own lips that she is
unable to make contact with her family and
was told by Desmond Ford that the reason
Pauline and Marina didn't meet was because
of Pauline having flu, another lie.'

'Pauline may not have wanted to see her
daughter after sustaining such a facial injury,'
Nick pointed out.

'Then why was an excuse given and not the
truth?' Erin argued. 'Added to that, Mark's
attitude was hostile toward me and it was clear
Pauline was frightened.'

'But was it of him?' Nick questioned.
'Perhaps they had just had a lovers' spat.'

'She was hiding her injury, Nick,' Erin said
as she left the window and went to stand by his.
desk. 'She wanted to know how Marina was—
in fact, she sounded desperate to know—but
she didn't want me to see what had happened
to her.'

Nick nodded slowly, his expression
thoughtful. 'What do you want to do? Inform

the police?'

'How can they intervene? It's probably classed as a domestic situation, besides which we have no proof. If Pauline had come to see me it might have been a different story. As it is, I have only my suspicions to go on.'

'Then I think it's time for me to call,' Nick said, and stood up.

'For what reason?' Erin frowned. 'Pauline's my patient. I should go, if anyone does.'

'But Mark is already aware of your interest,' Nick said as he looked down at her. 'I don't want you involved in a confrontation of any kind. Don't worry, I'll think of something plausible to say. Now, stop worrying and leave it to me.'

Erin felt his hand rest on her arm and she shivered, the warmth of his skin on hers making her look up and meet his eyes. She realised how relieved she was to be able to share her concerns with him. He gazed at her, and she felt drawn by the fierce attraction she had tried so hard to resist over the last few weeks.

'Th-thanks,' she mumbled, about to turn away, but Nick's fingers closed around her arm and she felt his powerful grip as she stared up at him.

'One more thing,' he said quietly as his mouth turned up into a slow smile. 'Saturday.'

She nodded uncertainly. 'What of it?'

'Your interview—what time is it?'

'One o'clock,' she answered, then felt a shudder run through her body as he raised a finger to lift a lock of hair which had fallen across her brow.

'How would you like a chauffeur for the day?' His tone was light, but she saw by the glimmer in his dark eyes that he meant what he'd said. 'Perhaps we could have dinner and catch a show, before driving home.'

She was on the point of refusing but his fingers still held her wrist in a gentle grasp as a small voice inside her head asked why not. The journey would be made more acceptable with company, and in truth she wasn't looking forward to the day's driving.

Nick's gaze remained on her and the warmth from his hand seemed to travel up her arm. She found herself hesitating that fraction of a second too long as he smiled and said, before she could speak, 'That's settled, then. Hopefully we'll have a fine day—according to the reports the weather is going to hold until next month.'

He released her and she took a breath, knowing that she was weak-willed enough to pose no objection to his offer, content for fate to lend a hand in what she had been anticipating as the culmination of all her plans.

*   *   *

The rest of the week passed without event,

though a major stumbling block was Nick's first visit to Pauline at Mark's flat. Nick was unable to gain entrance, with apparently no one at home to answer his call.

His second visit, though, on Friday resulted in a chat with the elderly lady who lived in the ground-floor flat. Nick revealed that he was a doctor in search of a patient, and she explained that there had been several disruptions of late between the nice older woman who was living with the young man in the flat on the first floor.

'Still not enough to add weight to our theory,' Nick said that evening as they left the surgery and walked to their cars.

'We just have to wait, in other words, until something happens?' Erin's voice was concerned, and although she knew that Nick had done his best she wasn't prepared to let the matter rest there.

'I don't know what else we can do,' Nick said reasonably, 'other than stake out the place and wait.'

'What about her job?' Erin said suddenly as she recalled that Pauline was a secretary. 'We could approach her there.'

'Is it on the records?' Nick's voice was doubtful.

'I'm sure it must be because of Marina.'

'It will be too late to do anything now, with tomorrow being Saturday. If she has Marina at weekends, no doubt she doesn't work then.'

'We'll just have to leave it until Monday,' Erin sighed as they reached their cars and she unlocked her door.

'As for tomorrow,' Nick reminded her swiftly, 'we'll leave at nine. That should give us plenty of time and we won't have to rush.'

She nodded, her heart racing as she met his stare. 'I'll be ready,' she told him, and as he turned to walk towards his car she felt a wave of excitement flow through her, a sensation she had been trying to deny all week long as she'd thought of being with him again.

*   *   *

Nick had been right about the weather. It was a beautiful September day, and the sky was clear of cloud as they set off next morning. Green fields and russet forest passed by until they reached the motorway and the uninterrupted journey towards the City.

As Erin watched him drive, she found herself glancing at the tanned forearms revealed under the rolled-up cuffs of his casual shirt, the electric blue cotton accentuating the dark and grainy texture of his skin. Downy hairs grew over his forearms and disappeared under the cloth, to reappear again at his throat where his shirt lay open at the top button. He had worn navy chinos that clung to his thighs as he sat, relaxed, at the wheel, and her eyes didn't miss the rise and fall of powerful muscle as he changed gear.

His dark hair had grown now and dipped just below the collar of his shirt, its glossy abundance swept back from his forehead. His eyes went every now and then to the driving mirror as he noted the traffic behind them. A CD of light classical music was playing and the strains of the music were just audible above their conversation.

Erin had decided to wear a smooth, silk dress in pale green. Its soft lines and calf-length hem seemed appropriate for the interview and for travelling in warm weather. She had draped a single row of pearls around her neck and her dark hair shone with gleaming highlights. At her ears, pearl earrings glimmered under the bob and she felt both comfortable and cool in the clothes she had chosen to wear.

Nick had stared at her in open admiration as she had opened the door to his ring, and she had flushed slightly at his complimentary words. The day lent itself to easy conversation and she felt that, other than the formality of the interview at the offices of the private clinic in Kensington, she would be able to relax and enjoy herself.

They had arranged to meet an hour after her interview at a restaurant they were both familiar with, and as Nick entered the outskirts of the City Erin silently prepared herself for what lay ahead.

It grew warmer as the traffic steadily thickened and Nick parked outside the City centre, taking a cab for the rest of their journey.

'See you later,' he said as they stood outside the block of impressive-looking Georgian houses. 'And good luck.'

She smiled as she stepped out onto the pavement and looked back. 'Thanks. I'll look forward to lunch.'

She watched the taxi move off, then, smoothing down her dress, she turned towards the flight of steps that led up to the impressive entrance. In a few minutes she was ensconced in a large reception room, awaiting the director of the clinic with whom she had been in contact over the last few months. Thankfully it was cool as she sat quietly, but the heat and noise of the City had already caused her to recall with some unease the world which she had decided to return to in the New Year.

Despite her sense of foreboding, the interview went well, and the prospect of a post in private practice seemed to have no obvious drawbacks other than the search for accommodation. That would come later, Erin reminded herself as she listened to the female director asking her whether she had considered the question and what her plans would be if she accepted the position.

Erin explained that for the first few months of the New Year she had tentatively arranged to stay at a friend's flat, and that seemed to satisfy her interviewer. However, as Erin took her leave and walked out into the cloying heat of the September day, she felt a chill inside. As she walked along the streets and past the elegant buildings with their leafy trees outside, she inhaled the strong odours of the City, tasting the emissions of the never-ending streams of traffic.

She recalled it all so well from her training days. The anticipation of life as a qualified doctor had filled her in the early years, yet at the back of her mind she had always yearned for the countryside and a rural lifestyle.

Now here she was once again, returning to the place she had tried so hard to leave. In time, she told herself, she would forget Hayford Minster and the dreams that had so cruelly eluded realisation, a dream which had been opened up for her by Max Darvill during her last year of training when Max had offered her a post at his small country practice when she qualified.

By then Max had made plans to establish a fully modernised medical centre, the one they now occupied. In conjunction with Alissa and Alec Rogers, they had successfully formed the Minster Practice, and Erin felt a warm flow of pleasure run through her as she recalled her delight at being a junior member of the partnership. When she had finally persuaded Simon to move from London and buy their dream home, her happiness had seemed complete. Until that day at the Minster . . . when she had waited and waited in her bridal gown . . . leaning on her father's arm . . . unable to believe that Simon would never arrive.

Erin approached the kerb, the traffic flowing busily past her. She swayed slightly, reaching out to steady herself on a lamppost. She hadn't let Simon's reluctance to change his lifestyle and move to the country stop her. She had been so desperate to achieve her dreams—a fact that Nick had pointed out to her a month before her wedding, a fact she had chosen to ignore.

She swayed again, her other hand going up to her eyes as the road swam in front of her and cars, faces, buildings all seemed to merge, a feeling of nausea sweeping through her.

It was only a strong hand around her waist, catching her as her knees gave way, that prevented her from falling. 'Lean on me,' Nick said as he caught her, his familiar voice close to her ear.

She nodded, allowing him to take her weight as the blood seemed to drain from her legs. She held tightly to him as he hailed a cab and they climbed into it. She sank onto the seat and took a breath, waiting until the sensation passed. Nick's arm was around her, and as he gave the driver instructions she felt the energy slowly return and the sickness drain away.

'I'm s-sorry,' she murmured as he waited quietly, his eyes studying her with concern. 'I'm all right now, really.'

'What happened?' he asked, his forehead pleated into a deep frown. 'For one moment I thought you were about to fall into the road.'

She sighed, leaning back against the cool leather, and gave a bewildered shrug. 'I think I'm just out of practice. The traffic, the noise, the heat of the day . . .'

'City life,' he murmured ruefully. 'You'll have to get used to it again. You've been living in the sticks for too long.'

She nodded. 'Yes, possibly.' She frowned as she looked up at him and asked curiously, 'What were you doing there? I thought you would be at the restaurant.'

'I was,' he told her as he looked into her eyes, 'but unfortunately it's closed for refurbishment so I came back to the clinic and hoped I'd be in time to meet you.'

She smiled weakly. 'Well, I'm glad you did.'

'Feeling better?' he asked, and she nodded, his fingers twisting into her own and giving them a squeeze.

She smiled, now feeling foolish. 'Much better, thanks.'

'I've told the taxi driver to take us somewhere closer,' he said quietly. 'We'll have a light lunch, then perhaps get some air in the park.'

'Yes, a walk sounds wonderful,' she agreed, and as she relaxed, she realised how relieved she was to be with him and that he was still holding her hand, the pressure of it increasing as he looked down at her and smiled.

*　　　*　　　*

A shower of light summer rain served to cool the heavy atmosphere, and when they emerged from the restaurant after a light salad lunch they strolled hand in hand through the park, content to talk and laugh and enjoy the day.

There was little they didn't discuss as they explored the park, then left to walk by the river, its surface reflecting the overcast sky. Time sped by as they joined the busy streets still packed with tourists. A few spots of rain fell as people found refuge in shops and cafés.

That evening they found a quiet little side street and, avoiding the crowds, ate freshly baked croissants and sipped Italian coffee.

'Do you feel like a show?' Nick asked as they prepared to leave, but Erin hesitated, unsure if that was what she really felt like doing. Normally she would have shown greater enthusiasm, but the day had been a long one and more than anything she felt like a shower and change of clothes.

'If that's what you'd like,' she answered as they stood in the narrow street. Glancing at one another, they laughed.

'It's been a long day,' he said, guessing her thoughts. 'What do you say to us returning to the car and making our way home? We can eat a meal on the way, and enjoy the journey without rushing.' He glanced up at the bruised-looking clouds that were hanging ominously above them. 'Besides which, if I'm not much mistaken it looks as though we may have a storm on the way.'

Having decided on that, they found a cab for the last time that day and made their way back to the car. It was as they transferred from one vehicle to another that they heard thunder roll in the distance. Rain spattered on the windscreen and freshened the air, as had the light shower that had broken the muggy heat earlier in the day. Darkness fell as they travelled south and a streak of lightning flashed across the sky. The storm, which had been threatening all day, finally broke.

The dry earth refused to absorb the downpour and Nick decreased speed on the motorway as vehicle lights dazzled against the reflection of wet tarmac. Spray cascaded up on either side of them and there were warnings of heavy rain flashing across the motorway signs.

'I think we should turn off the motorway up here if we want to eat,' Nick muttered as he frowned ahead through the driving rain.

Erin shivered as they slowed down to change lanes. Turning to him, she shrugged lightly. 'We're almost there. Why don't we eat at my flat? I've something in the fridge—a lasagne and salad. How does that sound?'

He turned briefly to her, his expression surprised. 'Are you sure?'

She nodded. 'We can watch the storm wear itself out while we eat.' She laughed softly. 'Somehow it seems a pity to go inside a restaurant and ignore it.'

'I can go along with that.' He grinned. Signalling to return to the offside lane, they travelled on towards home.

CHAPTER NINE

They said very little as they sat at the table and shared the simple meal by candlelight, watching the storm through the window-panes as it passed over the Minster tower. The rain beat down on the small balcony outside, drumming on the wrought-iron balustrade that led off the long windows. It made a breathtaking scene and one which Erin knew she would never forget, the lights of the ancient building reflecting up against the gun-metal sky, a relief that could almost have been taken from the pages of a picture book.

'So, what are your plans for the future?' Nick asked as he leaned on the table, pushing his empty plate to one side.

'At the clinic?' she asked, knowing that eventually they would have to discuss this subject, one they had managed to avoid all day.

He nodded. 'Was the interview successful?'

She also leaned forward, unable to finish the last of her *crème caramel*, her fingers playing with the rim of the plate, turning it slowly as she hesitated. 'Successful in the sense that I have agreed to start in February when there will be a vacancy.'

Nick nodded slowly, for a moment silent. 'Private practice . . .' he murmured thoughtfully. 'Quite a change.'

'Yes,' she acknowledged, 'though the clinic is run much as it is here. They have practitioners for complementary therapies, just as we have, and there are five MDs not four, two of whom are female. The doctor I'm to replace will be on maternity leave.'

He caught her eye as she looked up, his brow creased in a light frown. 'Your mind is made up, then?' he asked softly. 'You are leaving?'

'Yes,' Erin said quietly. 'In the New Year.'

'And you say Simon Forester has nothing to do with your decision?' he persisted, unwilling to let her evade his gaze.

'No, of course not,' she answered, a little too quickly.

'But why return to the City?' he continued, one eyebrow shooting up. 'It was the place you were so eager to leave once. Are you sure that after his visit recently . . .' His sentence ended on a questioning note and it was a few seconds before Erin realised what he was saying.

'You think I've decided to go back because of Simon being there?' Erin said in a shocked voice.

'Why not?' Nick lifted his shoulders and leaned back in his chair. 'It's quite possible, even though you won't admit it to yourself.'

She was about to say that the thought had never crossed her mind when the telephone rang. She sighed, standing up to answer it at the extension on the small table by the fire. It was a friend who asked her if she would like to meet one evening at the sports centre for a game of squash. Having made an arrangement for mid-week, Erin said goodbye, aware that her response had been clipped and rather cool.

She hadn't meant it to sound that way, but she was still involved in her conversation with Nick. Turning back to him, she found he was staring at her, his eyes dark and thoughtful, an expression in them she was unable to translate.

'I enjoyed being with you today,' he said quietly, 'and I don't want to spoil the evening . . .'

Erin nodded slowly, her green eyes lifting to his. 'It was good to have you with me.'

'And if I don't leave here soon,' he said as he stood up and walked towards her, 'I won't want to leave at all.'

160

She knew that he was giving her the opportunity to end the evening, and she also knew that she should take it, but she didn't want the evening to end or the moment to come when they would say goodnight.

What she did want was to be taken into his arms and to be kissed, and as he leaned forward, raising his fingers to lift a lock of hair from her cheek and tuck it behind her ear, she took a breath, her heart beginning to pound as he hesitated for one brief second.

'Do you *want* me to go?' he asked softly.

Unable to take her eyes from his, she shook her head, her lips parting as he tilted her chin, his mouth coming down softly to hers, the moment of enquiry brief as she slid her hands around his neck and he took her into his arms.

'Erin . . .' he whispered, and then she was lost as the sound of the rain continued a low drumming beyond the beating of her heart. She lost all sense of time as his kiss deepened, her chest rising and falling rapidly as she responded, knowing that this was what she had wanted and that nothing could stop what was about to happen.

He moved down, his lips brushing against the slope of her neck, her breastbone and the smooth skin that was hidden below the neckline of her dress. Sliding his fingers over the small buttons, he released them and moved his hand across the swell of her breasts. She arched involuntarily, the yearning inside her growing with each movement. When he stopped, raising his head to look questioningly into her eyes, she knew that she was lost and that whatever was destined to be was now out of her control.

In silence they walked to her bedroom and he closed the door behind them, holding her shoulders for a second before sliding her dress downwards, slipping the buttons one by one until it fell to the floor in a pool of silk at her feet.

He stared at her, his eyes going slowly over her, taking in the swell of her breasts under the ivory bra and the petticoat with its wafer-thin straps and trimming of lace. In a gentle movement he slid this from her shoulders and unfastened the bra as she gazed up at him, the fleeting moment of self-consciousness passing as he lowered his head to kiss her again.

She leaned against him, shivering at his touch, and her fingers moved of their own accord, hastening with each movement, undoing the buttons of his shirt and finally letting the soft blue cloth fall to the floor.

His skin was smooth and tanned and in the soft light of the bedroom he looked so tall and handsome that she almost stopped breathing as she took in the beauty of his bare torso. The fine black hairs, which she had noticed on his arms as he drove, grew in abundance over his chest, a downy forest of curling, masculine hair that tapered into an arrowhead and disappeared below the slim leather belt at his waist.

She realised that she stood in only her briefs, a silky pair of ivory lace, and he lifted her into his arms, laying her on the wide double bed, sliding the duvet away as she fell back against the white pillows, her hair spilling across one of them like a chestnut halo. He stood above her, gazing down, until she saw him swallow, slide away his belt and join her, almost naked, on the bed.

For just a moment she recalled the last time she had made love, yearning to be loved by Simon in the way she'd needed and consoling herself that his attitude towards sex wasn't always as selfish, that he'd probably been tired and exhausted from his journey down from the City and that, as she'd lain unfulfilled beside him as he'd slept, when they were married their understanding of one another would deepen.

Now she knew how wrong that match would have been, how disastrous a union they would have made. Instinct told her, as Nick leaned to caress her, his mouth lingering on her trembling lips, teasing and biting gently, that this would be different.

She was panting with desire, her body shuddering as Nick's fingers removed the last garment, sliding the soft silk of her panties over her thighs. She responded, pushing the cotton band of his shorts over the hard muscle

163

that tensed at her touch.

She moved down, her tongue flicking across his chest, brushing his stomach as he had so sensuously brushed hers a moment ago, heightening all her sensations to a quivering pitch, her mouth open in anticipation as his lips found hers again. He lifted her on top of him and she moaned aloud, his manhood startling and delighting her.

For a moment the thought came to her that they had taken no precautions and he, too, seemed to hesitate, but their need was overwhelming and, all sensible reasoning abandoned, she allowed herself to forget everything but the moment.

Then she was beneath him, his lips exploring her, his hands caressing her breasts and firm nipples. She sighed, expelling a breath of deep desire, then inhaling quickly as he sensed that need, moving down to repeat the pleasures of his darting tongue and sensual touch.

Her hands were twisting in his hair, the feel of the texture and thickness sending a shiver over her, her body tensing with exquisite pleasure as he entered her. With an urgency that matched her own he moved upwards, claiming her mouth, their bodies moving in rhythm until he brought her to a shuddering climax.

The rain was still beating against the window as they sank beside one another, arms and legs entwined, bodies replete from their lovemaking. Without a word he turned towards her and lifted her hand, laying it back on the pillow and stroking the skin between her fingers as he gazed into her eyes.

No words were needed as they lay there, the storm outside still raging as she moved closer and laid her head against his chest. She wanted to hear his heart, to listen to the life-giving beat that had thundered through her as they'd come to that climax, to know that all this was real and perfect and that she hadn't imagined it.

As though sensing her need, he drew her towards him, wrapping his arms around her, kissing her hair. Their bodies were damp, their skin sensitive to touch still, and she shivered, allowing the after-sensations to ripple through her as tiredness finally lowered her lids and her eyes closed.

The last thing she remembered was the sheet being drawn over her, her arm across his waist and a distant roll of thunder echoing across the night sky.

*   *   *

Erin awoke to the ringing of the telephone and the movement of the body lying beside her as she blinked, vaguely aware of Nick's hand sweeping the empty surface of the pine cabinet beside him, a reflex action that Erin recognised only too well from her own startled awakenings.

'It's on this side,' she murmured as she came awake, smiling at his confusion in the unfamiliar surroundings as he sat up, thrusting back the hair that had fallen over his forehead. He grinned and she reached for the telephone, sliding the sheet around her as she leaned onto the pillow with one elbow, blinking the sleep from her eyes.

'Erin, sorry to disturb you. It's Max,' she heard as she came fully awake. 'I'm at the hospital. I'm afraid I was called to one of your patients about an hour ago. There had been some sort of domestic upheaval—her name is Pauline Ford.'

Erin sat up quickly. 'Pauline Ford—yes. What's happened, Max?'

'One of her neighbours phoned and explained that they'd found her in a collapsed state at the bottom of a flight of stairs. She refused to go to hospital, but she agreed to them calling her GP and, as you know, I'm on call. When I arrived there she was in the neighbour's flat, still very confused and with a bump on her head that indicated she might have been suffering from concussion. However, there were other marks on her face and she said that they were also from a fall and that you knew about them.'

'I know about them only because I happened to meet her in a supermarket,' Erin explained quickly. 'In fact, I've been trying to contact her ever since. She had quite a nasty black eye and, though she said it was a fall, I'm afraid I found that hard to accept.'

'Yes, me, too,' Max agreed. 'Well, now she says that she fell down the flight of stairs that leads up to the flat in which she lives. The police were called in by the neighbour who heard the disturbance—apparently not the first, it appears. You may have a visit from them today so I'm phoning to prepare you.'

'All right. Thank you, Max. What is Pauline's condition at the moment?' she asked as she glanced quickly at Nick beside her.

'They are keeping her under observation for a day or two,' Max told her. 'She says she can't remember very much at all, only that she lost her footing and blacked out. She doesn't know for how long and she's pretty bruised, but there are no breaks, luckily enough.'

Erin sank back against the pillow. 'Will you tell Pauline that I'll be in to see her later in the day?'

Max said that he would and Erin replaced the phone, turning slowly back to Nick. He was looking at her with a deep frown as she repeated what Max had just told her.

After she had finished, Nick slid his arm under the sheet and around her waist, one dark eyebrow hitched up as he sighed. 'Do you want me to go before the police arrive?' he asked.

'Max wasn't sure when they would call.' She

167

leaned towards him, a smile tugging at the corners of her lips. 'And, anyway, why should I want you to leave?'

He pulled a face, his smile rueful. 'It's rather early—I don't think by any stretch of the imagination I could explain being here as a professional visit.'

'What about a social one?' Erin teased.

'You're serious?' He pulled her towards him, stroking back her hair with the palms of his hands.

She nodded. 'Yes, I'm serious. I'm sure the police have more serious things to be concerned about.'

'Like, how did Pauline sustain her injuries, for instance?' Nick sighed as he enfolded her gently against his chest.

'I think we both know the answer to that,' Erin said as she lay beside him, aware of the dark brown lustre of his eyes under their fringe of dark lashes.

They gazed at each other for a moment and then he pulled her closer, the smile he gave her leaving her in no doubt that, despite the threatened ring of the doorbell, he was in no hurry to rise and, she realised, neither was she.

*   *   *

Two uniformed police officers called at ten-thirty, by which time both Erin and Nick had showered, dressed and breakfasted. They

168

confirmed that Pauline Ford and Desmond Ford were their patients and gave what information they could, though Erin was obliged to admit that Pauline had never attended the surgery for examination of physical injuries.

Her patient had refused to say anything other than she had fallen down the stairs in the early hours of the morning and could remember no more. Whether she really couldn't recall what had happened or whether she was deliberately refusing to co-operate with the police was a question left unanswered as the officers took their leave.

'I think she's covering up for Mark,' Erin sighed, as she closed the door and bent down to the table to pick up four empty coffee-cups. 'And I think they think that, too, but they can't prove it.'

'You think he's a violent man?' Nick leaned thoughtfully against the door-frame, frowning at her. He was wearing the same shirt and trousers he'd worn last night, his dark hair still damp from a shower, and Erin felt her heart race as she looked at him, suddenly aware that they were alone for the first time after spending the night together.

'I think it's possible.' She nodded. 'I know he works at a bar and keeps late hours and that the neighbour apparently has heard a disturbance on more than one occasion. I know that Pauline was afraid to talk to me in the supermarket and I know that he was hostile towards me. Adding all these things up, I think there's every chance that she's probably protecting him.'

Nick's face darkened, and, thrusting his hands into his pockets, he sighed, chewing on his lip. 'Would you mind if I came with you to see her?' he asked quietly.

Erin walked towards him, coffee-cups balanced in her hands. 'No . . . although I'm not sure if she'll want to see either of us.'

'We'll take a gamble, shall we? No harm done if she won't talk to us.' His tone was light as, removing the china from her hands, he placed it on the mantelpiece then turned towards her. Softly running his hands over the soft pink sweater she wore, he drew her to him, hugging her closely. 'We've had no chance to talk about . . . us,' he said as she laid her cheek against his chest. 'No regrets?'

'You mean . . . about us?' Her voice was husky as she closed her eyes and inhaled his familiar scent, non-cosmetic and very male.

'Yes, of course I mean us.' He lifted her chin and gazed into her eyes.

And Erin knew that she had no regrets, not even the smallest, and that for the moment she wasn't thinking of the past or the future, only of the present and the man with whom, last night, she had made indescribably fulfilling love. But before she could reply, his mouth came down hard on hers, receiving a response that left him in no doubt as to her answer.

*   *   *

'A fractured rib and facial bruising, but Doctor was more concerned about the length of time she was unconscious,' the sister said as Nick and Erin stood in the small ward office. 'We're going to keep her under observation and Doctor will see her again tomorrow. We've put her in a side ward for the moment as we had one free.'

Erin wasn't surprised to find Pauline tearful and distressed, and as she glanced at Nick as they entered the room it was clear that the look Pauline gave them was fearful. Her face was swollen and her lip stitched, the earlier bruising still evident on her cheek and jaw, and Erin felt her heart sink as she recognised that Pauline was a victim of physical abuse.

The conversation was limited to what Pauline could remember of the fall, which was very little. She had been alone, she said, and thought she had tripped over the carpeting at the top of the stairs. When Nick asked if Mark had been there, she shook her head, saying that he hadn't returned from his shift.

They stayed only a short while since it was obviously an effort for Pauline to talk, but Nick and Erin paused in the corridor outside.

'She didn't mention any disturbance, unlike the neighbour who was woken by it,' Nick said,

171

speaking aloud Erin's own thoughts.

'The police can hardly do anything if she won't tell them the truth,' Erin sighed, 'although it seems obvious what really happened.'

As they were standing there a figure approached, and Erin turned to see Desmond Ford hurrying towards them. He was clearly upset and when he reached them his gaze went over Erin's shoulder to the side ward.

'Is Pauline all right?' His voice was shaking as he thrust a hand through his untidy dark hair. He looked dishevelled and had obviously not shaved. 'What happened? Is my wife in there?'

Nick grasped his arm as the agitated man pushed past them. In a firm tone Nick said, 'You shouldn't see her until you've calmed down. Come and have a cup of tea first.' Nick glanced at Erin and she nodded.

'The coffee-bar is probably open for visitors,' Erin suggested, realising that Desmond would only upset Pauline if he went in there now.

Nick slid his hand to Desmond's back. 'Come on, we'll come with you.'

Desmond hesitated, reluctant to be dissuaded from entering the side ward, but Nick's firm gesture prevented him from doing so and a few moments later they were, all three, sitting around a table in the hospital's coffee-shop.

'How did you know that Pauline was here?' Nick asked.

'Marina rang her mother, hoping to speak to her on the public telephone at the flats. She hadn't seen Pauline for some while and wanted me to take her over there today. However, it wasn't Pauline who answered the phone but a neighbour. Marina handed me the telephone and I couldn't believe what I heard next. I asked my housekeeper to stay with Marina while I came here to see for myself.' He looked up then, his eyes fixed on their faces as though he couldn't believe what was happening. 'Is it true?' he demanded. 'Was Pauline assaulted?'

'We don't know,' Erin said quietly. 'It seems your wife fell down the stairs at the flat but she doesn't recall very much other than that.'

'But you think it was *him,* don't you?' Desmond's face was suddenly furious, his fists clenched on the table. 'You must, otherwise you wouldn't be here—'

'Whatever happened,' Nick interrupted calmly, 'your wife is feeling very low and extremely vulnerable. You should take this into account before you speak to her. You'll be shocked at the bruising on her face, but try not to be alarmed. She's going to recover and you must keep that in mind.' He added carefully, 'You know, she will need somewhere to recuperate. I think she might welcome the offer of somewhere to stay, but only if she isn't subjected to an inquisition. She's already had

173

one from the police and obviously the hospital staff.'

'You mean you think she might come home?' Desmond's eyes suddenly came back into focus as he attempted to control his anger.

'Isn't it worth a try?' Nick stirred his coffee slowly. 'The situation could be turned your advantage, Desmond, if handled well enough. That is, if you still want your marriage to survive.'

A mixture of emotions filled the distraught man's face and Erin watched with sadness as she saw him try to come to terms with the situation. But she also saw something else there, too, a compassion and a tiny flicker of hope at Nick's words.

After a few moments Desmond swallowed and sank back against the chair, resting his hands on the table with a sigh. 'I still love her,' he said brokenly. 'But will that be enough?' He shook his head slowly as he stared up at them. 'How in heaven's name have we come to this . . . my wife beaten up in hospital, our daughter motherless and our lives together in ruins?'

*　　　*　　　*

The Minster tower was hidden by a fine September mist as Erin stared out, inhaling the breeze that trickled in through the window and couldn't be mistaken for any other season's scent. Nick stood behind her, his arms wrapped around her waist, his chin touching the top of her head as she relaxed against him.

It had been a confused Sunday, with no apparent resolution to Desmond's and Pauline's problems, although when they had left Desmond he had been calmer and had gone in to see his wife, controlling the anger and resentment he still felt.

The Fords had not been an easy subject to dismiss, and though Nick and Erin had gone for a walk in the countryside they had resumed the threads of their conversation about the Fords throughout supper at Erin's flat.

Now, with the evening drawing in around them, they seemed not to want to talk anymore, and Erin turned in his arms and slid her hands along his shoulders. She looked up into his face and saw the yearning in his eyes, the emotion that also filled her, as she shuddered softly against him. She wanted him and she knew he wanted her but, restraining himself, he kissed her questioningly, the intention behind his kiss being to allow her to claim her own space and time if she wished.

But she didn't want to end the day without him, and as she thought of her bedroom she knew it would be a lonely place without him lying beside her. She wanted his kisses and his lovemaking and she knew that she also needed to be reassured, something deep inside her relating to the distress of her patient earlier that day.

175

Simon had never raised a hand to her, but the pain and humiliation she had suffered at his public rejection had not been unlike a physical battering, and when she had seen Pauline in hospital her heart had twisted involuntarily at the pitiful sight.

Erin gazed up into Nick's face and saw tenderness and longing and knew that it must reflect her own, a chemistry which had begun long ago when she had first met him. Had she not been loyal to Simon, she might have questioned her feelings then for a man who had not loved her and known that what she'd felt for Nick had been entirely different.

'Let's go to bed,' he whispered as she lifted her hands to rest on the powerful arch of his neck and stroked with her fingertips the sensual curve that dipped down to his chest. His voice was rough with need and she knew that his question was asked with a barely contained control as his arms tightened around her and his mouth came down hungrily on hers.

CHAPTER TEN

On a Friday evening late in September Alissa stood thoughtfully in her kitchen as she replaced the phone and tucked the opened letter from Sweden behind it.

176

Had she done right in giving Nick's telephone number to Sherry? she wondered. Sherry had said that she'd mislaid it, which seemed reasonable enough, but even so Alissa was troubled. Sherry had said that she was coming over from America and that she was hoping to call in to see Nick, a visit that could only bring unhappiness for Erin, she realised. Then there was the question of Kirsten and the letter from Sweden which would ultimately resolve another issue if Max agreed.

As she prepared the evening meal for the family, she smiled as Max entered the kitchen with Jake in his arms. 'Hi, there,' he called as Jake helpfully released the knot of his tie and drooled over his clean white shirt. 'Supper almost ready?' Max asked hungrily, still dressed in his dark suit as he peered across the kitchen at the saucepans on the range and inhaled the delicious aroma. 'Pasta?' he guessed correctly.

Alissa grinned as she nodded. 'Five minutes more, that's all. Are the children ready to eat?'

Max nodded, climbing onto a stool at the breakfast bar and bouncing Jake in his arms. 'Aaron's doing his prep upstairs, Bas and Sasha are in the study, working on a project for Christmas. And, as you can see, Jake is attempting to eat my tie for supper!'

Alissa smiled as she watched her small son attempt to stuff the pure silk tie into his mouth, prevented only by Max's firm resistance to the idea. Turning from the range, she walked to the table, a frown slowly spreading over her forehead. Max, dispensing with the tie completely, slid Jake's small legs into the high chair.

'Talking of Christmas,' Alissa murmured as she watched the large hands of her husband settle Jake comfortably, 'it isn't so very far off now . . .'

Max lifted his eyebrows ruefully. 'And . . .?'

'Well . . . I was wondering . . . did you have the practice meeting eventually?'

Max nodded. 'As you know, we had one scheduled for last week after Erin's trip to London, but Kirstie cancelled because some of the nursing staff had flu so we finally got around to it on Wednesday. I'm afraid Erin's still of the same mind. She plans to leave for London in January, so any time before the New Year . . .'

'We need a locum?'

'We certainly do.'

'And Kirstie hasn't come up with anyone yet?'

''Fraid not.' Max frowned curiously at his wife as he turned towards her. 'Do you have someone in mind?'

Alissa smiled, bending down to tickle Jake's pink chin. 'I might have.'

'Anyone I know?' Max's tone was intrigued.

'Oh, yes . . .' Alissa crooked an eyebrow. 'I had a letter today from Astrid.'

178

'Sasha's last au pair?' Max queried.

Alissa nodded. 'As you know, Astrid's training to be a linguist, which was one reason we were lucky enough to have her stay with us for so long when we first moved to Hayford Minster. And now her younger sister, Kirsten, wants to come to England and study for a year. She stayed with us in the holidays several times. She's a sweet girl and—'

'You mean you're thinking of coming back to work sooner than planned?' Max interrupted with amusement in his voice. 'Now, why is it that I'm not surprised?'

Alissa smiled and walked over to her husband and young son, sliding her arms around them. 'Well, what do you think of the idea?'

'Are you sure that's what you'd like to do?' Max asked as the little boy cooed happily between them.

Alissa shrugged easily. 'Well, it's been almost a year now since I stopped work. I think I can fit in a few hours each week, providing I've someone reliable to help with Jake.' If she was honest with herself, she was more than ready to take up her place at the surgery again, and who better to look after Jake than Kirsten, someone whom she knew and would trust?

'When does Kirsten plan to come to England?' Max asked.

'She's free to come now, so Astrid writes. I'm sure there will be no problem as regards dates.'

'In which case, Alec could still help us out over Christmas, but not to the extent that he would be under any pressure,' Max murmured thoughtfully. 'He seems to be coping well on his present medication. I don't think a few hours would be out of the question, certainly if he shared the surgeries with you.' Max nodded slowly. 'And you're sure that's what you want, darling?'

Alissa smiled, a small sigh escaping her lips. 'I just wish Erin would stay on with us. We all work so well together and I'll miss her but, then, she does seem to have her heart set on leaving, and I suppose if that's really what she wants . . .'

Max was already shaking his head. 'As a matter of fact, I don't think it is. Somehow I get the impression that she's not as happy about the idea as she tries to make out.'

It was a comment which left Alissa deep in thought as she returned to the range to stir the sauce, her forehead creased in a thoughtful frown. She had hoped that Nick's presence in Erin's life might alter the course she had chosen to take—was it too late, she wondered, for this to happen? And then she thought of Sherry again and the faint glimmer of hope faded.

As the children could be heard coming noisily down the stairs, Alissa found herself wondering if Sherry's telephone call indicated that she was about to walk into Nick's life once more, and Alissa suspected this could only mean one thing—that Nick still hadn't severed the ties that bound him to a very determined woman.

*   *   *

'So, what has been happening, Tom?' Erin probed gently as she sat beside Tom Knight in the nursing home where he was staying while his wife had her hip operation. 'How is Gladys?'

'They tell me she's fine,' said Tom, his lined face confused. 'The trouble is, they won't let me go and see her.'

'You will be able to shortly, just as soon as she's over the operation,' Erin assured him. 'Now, could I just have a listen to that wheeze of yours? I understand you've had some restless nights?'

Tom coughed, allowing Erin to open his shirt and place the stethoscope on his chest. She didn't like what she heard and was aware that the bout of flu had resulted in bronchitis. 'We'll have to give you a little more antibiotic,' she decided, 'and try to clear the small problem there.'

'Don't want anything. Just want to see Gladys,' Tom said morosely. 'I don't like this hotel. It's more like a prison.'

'It won't be for long,' Erin said, and watched

181

sadly as the old man drifted off into his own world. He had grown very confused during the last few weeks and there was no doubt that Gladys wouldn't be able to cope when she arrived home. Long-term care for Tom was inevitable, even though Gladys would protest fiercely against it.

Erin left the nursing home with a feeling of dismay and frustration. There was no cure for the dementia that had stricken Tom. All that could be done was to help Gladys in her hip replacement recovery and enable her to visit him when she was feeling stronger. The visits, though, would be dramatic. Tom would demand to be set free or not know his wife, more often than not refuse to communicate at all. The terrible disease was unpredictable and very emotionally exhausting for both carer and sufferer.

Placing Tom's notes in her bag, Erin drove on to her next call, attempting to put the Knights' problems to the back of her mind. She hadn't seen Mathew Sibson for some weeks and then it had only been for a few brief minutes when he'd arrived at surgery to collect a prescription. Erin found the small ground-floor flat in a new block just outside the town centre, but as she was about to knock the door opened and she recognised Gemma, the girl whom Mathew had introduced as his fiancée at the Lady Jayne.

'Oh, hello,' Gemma said sharply. 'Matt's in

the bedroom. I'm just leaving.'

Erin smiled and walked in, turning to speak to Gemma, but the girl was heading off down the hallway and didn't stop or look back. Erin closed the door and made her way to the bedroom, where she found Mathew propped up in bed, cushions behind his head and under his left leg.

'I hope you're not going to give me a ticking-off, too,' Mathew said dully.

Erin frowned at his new injury. 'What have you done, Mathew?'

He raised his eyebrows and sighed. 'I was daft enough to get in the way of a reversing car,' he said with a sigh. 'It didn't hurt me, but as I jumped out of the way I twisted my ankle.'

'When was this?' Erin sat down and began to unwind the bandage wrapped around his ankle and shin.

'Sunday afternoon.'

'You didn't go to Casualty?'

Mathew shook his head. 'It didn't seem too bad then. But today it's really painful, so much so I couldn't go into work. Gemma's dad was none too pleased, I can tell you.'

Erin examined the swelling around the ankle and drew a gasp from Mathew as she gently moved his toes. 'I think you'll have to have some X-rays,' Erin decided. 'You say you just twisted it?'

Mathew's face reddened. 'Well, I got it trapped for a few seconds, but it was nothing.

One of the mechanics saw what was happening and pushed me out of the way.'

'Mechanics?' Erin raised her eyebrows. 'You were at a race meeting?'

Mathew nodded. 'It was just a one-off, though,' he said quickly, his eyes not meeting hers. 'I was filling in for someone else who hadn't turned up.'

'Does Gemma know?' Erin thought she already knew the answer to that question and Mathew nodded miserably.

'I had to tell her in the end—well, with my ankle blown up like a balloon I had no alternative.'

'I see,' Erin said as she drew out a form from her case and began to fill it in. 'Have you got someone who can take you for an X-ray?'

Mathew nodded. 'Yes, no problem. Do you think something's broken?'

Erin shook her head. 'No, I don't, but it's best to make sure. Now, I'll prescribe something for pain relief. And, of course, it goes without saying you'll need rest.'

'And a sick note, I suppose,' Mathew added glumly. 'That won't go down too well with Gemma's dad. As a matter of fact, Gemma's just said that we might as well call off our engagement. She says that I don't really want to give up racing.'

'Is she right?' Erin asked with a frown.

'I want Gemma and I want to race,' Mathew answered candidly. 'But I know I can't have

184

both.'

Erin thought of how she had tried to persuade Simon into a lifestyle that she had wanted. In fact, she had almost taken it for granted that he would adjust to country life after they were married—a fact that Nick had been swift to point out to her at the time and which she had chosen to ignore.

She wished now that she could turn back the clock and thus save them both the pain and humiliation which had followed. But she had learned from her experience and she hoped that Mathew would make the right choice, although as she slid the clips on her case and saw the expression in her patient's eyes she couldn't help but feel sorry for the girl. Mathew's true love was speed—there was really no contest.

Erin drove home past the Fords' house that Tuesday evening and, to her surprise, saw Desmond and Marina walking towards the gate. She slowed the car and Marina, recognising her, waved. Pulling into the kerb, Erin turned off the engine and climbed out.

'Hello, Dr Brooks,' Desmond called as, hand in hand with his daughter, he walked towards Erin. 'What are you doing around this neck of the woods?'

'I've just made a house visit close by,' Erin said, smiling. 'And how are you now, Marina?'

'Oh, I'm fine, thank you, Dr Brooks. I've just been to dancing class.'

Erin raised her eyebrows. 'That sounds like fun. I didn't know you went. What sort of dancing is it?'

'Tap and ballet,' said Marina shyly. 'It's only my second class. Mummy took me last week but she's cooking supper tonight so Daddy came.'

Erin glanced at Desmond who bent down and said gently to his daughter, 'I'll just have a word with Dr Brooks, Marina. Run along in and tell Mummy that I shan't be long.'

Marina said goodbye and ran up the drive, her plaits bobbing on her shoulders. Desmond Ford looked at Erin. 'As you've probably gathered, Pauline is at home with us,' he explained. 'We had time to talk while she was in hospital and I thought about what Dr Hanson said. It seemed good advice after I'd cooled down. The upshot is that Pauline agreed to come back here after she was discharged.' He paused, shrugging slightly. 'I don't know what will happen—we're just taking one day at a time and trying to work things out.'

Erin was aware that Desmond was trying his best to pull the marriage together and she hoped for Marina's sake that the couple would be able to put the past behind them. It wouldn't be easy, she realised, for Pauline to forget Mark, despite the memories of the traumatic relationship she had shared with him. Erin had treated other such victims of violent behaviour and had come to realise that there was no guarantee of happiness once the truth was out. Some women drifted back into the relationship, unable to detach themselves. She just hoped that Pauline wasn't one of these and would find her way back to her family.

'If there's anything I can do, please, come and see me,' she said and Desmond nodded.

'I think my wife will need a check-up soon,' he added hesitantly. 'I'll tell her I've spoken to you.'

Erin smiled. 'Goodnight, Mr Ford . . . and good luck.'

He returned her smile, though Erin could see that it was an effort for him. 'Goodnight, Dr Brooks.'

As Erin drove home, she felt relieved that she had seen Desmond and at least knew that Pauline was for the moment in no danger. The evening had drawn in, with no early October sparkle, but her pulse raced slightly as she drew up outside the flats and saw that Nick was home.

Light spilled from his windows and as she climbed out of the car she realised that she ached to be in his arms. She paused as a thrill went through her at the thought of their lovemaking. Nick was a considerate lover and his desire to see her fulfilled touched her during their nights spent together, either in her flat or his.

He had made no reference to her departure in the New Year or to the phone call that had come through one day from Sherry while Erin had been with him. As she walked towards his door, a pang of unease gripped her at the memory of that awkward moment. Nick had shrugged after he had replaced the telephone, saying that Sherry was visiting England, but his reaction had been as though it was something that barely concerned him.

Erin tried to pull herself together as she knocked lightly, but a fleeting recollection flashed through her mind of the portfolio of photographs which had revealed Sherry as a beautiful and desirable woman. She had played an important role in his life—how could he possibly forget her?

The door opened and Nick stood there, casually dressed in jeans and sweatshirt. As if sensing her unease, he drew her into his arms, kissing her deeply, the moment needing no words.

As his lips moved passionately over hers, she decided not to think about the woman who had stared out at her from those pages and who might be about to reappear in his life. For now, this was all that mattered, his strong arms enfolding her against him, his kisses sweet and tender . . . and, blissfully, they had the whole night ahead of them to share.

*   *   *

'It's stunning, Fergus!' Erin stood with Nick in the artist's studio, gazing at the family portrait of the Darvills. 'Though I feel that's a rather inadequate description of your skilful work,' she added as she took a breath and exhaled in wonder as she gazed at the canvas.

'Do you think your friends, the Darvills, will like it?' Fergus frowned critically at the painting of Max and Alissa and their four children assembled in a family group, as Nick had photographed them. Fergus's golden eyebrows pleated into a frown. He had paint spattered over his woolly jumper and cords and his fair hair, streaked with grey, was tied back from his blond beard, making him look like the proverbial artist.

'There's no doubt of that,' Nick answered emphatically. 'When will it be finished, do you think?'

Fergus strode across his studio floor and picked up a gilt frame, bringing it back to place around the painting. 'Just this to add, and the final glaze. If you're happy with the finished article, shall we say a week to ten days?'

'That's fine,' Nick agreed at once. 'I'll ring you to confirm it.'

On their way out of the cottage Erin saw a number of paintings standing in rows along the hall, and Fergus explained that these were commissions yet to be completed.

Although she would have liked to have

studied them, Fergus seemed to be in a hurry and soon they were out at the car, Nick opening the door for her.

'Well, what do you think?' Nick started the car and reversed into the leafy road of the New Forest village. 'Do you like it?'

'Very much,' Erin acknowledged as he drove off. 'Fergus has captured something yet I don't quite know what it is.'

'Happiness, I think,' ventured Nick simply. 'Max and Alissa, the kids—they just look happy, an ingredient that seems to shine out from their faces.'

Erin felt a moment's pang of regret that her life without children, without the focus of the happiness that family life brought with it, was missing from her existence. That was what she regretted most from her wasted years with Simon. But the moment passed as she reminded herself that it didn't do to dwell on the past and that the present was all she could ever wish it to be as Nick reached out for her hand and squeezed it, murmuring softly, 'As we're out this way, let's take a walk down memory lane, shall we?'

He meant, as she knew, a visit to their special place which they had first visited together over sixteen months ago, though their next visit in July, she recalled, had been cut short by unhappy memories of the past.

But all that was changed today and she smiled, catching Nick's glance as he indicated to take the winding lane to their left. She felt very close to the man sitting beside her, his hands firmly clasped on the steering-wheel, his head tilted slightly in the way that was now so familiar to her. Leaning back, she drew in a soft breath and watched as the heart of the forest opened up to them.

The deciduous trees were turning a golden brown, while the rows of thick pine on either side of them were broken only by the five-barred gates which led to their dark interior. Occasionally a pony or two would cross the road and the cars would halt to allow them to cross safely. At one point Erin glimpsed a deer, making its way into the thick undergrowth, and it wasn't long before her heart began to race as she saw the familiar sign which had once announced that Briar House Hotel was under new management.

Now the sign, had been repainted and, though there were no longer baskets of brightly coloured flowers hanging outside, the white walls and leaded windows gleamed in the October sunshine.

'We're in time for lunch,' Nick said as they climbed out of the car and entered the low-beamed reception area. 'I'll reserve a table for two. Shall we have a drink in the bar beforehand?'

Erin nodded. 'That will be lovely.

She took the opportunity to use the cloakroom mirror and repair her make-up, refreshing her lipstick and brushing her hair. She looked in the mirror at her reflection, seeing the same tall, slender, chestnut-haired figure that had gazed out at her last year, two weeks before her wedding to Simon.

How could so much have happened in that space of time? And how different she felt now as she gazed at the green eyes regarding her, their depths glimmering with an expression that was hard to define, one that had never been there before. But, then, she had never felt this way with Simon and, looking back, she wondered how she would have ever coped with that realisation after their marriage.

Nick had already found a seat in the cosy lounge bar, and when Erin took her place beside him they ordered fruit juices, relaxing against one another as they listened to the softly piped music. Nick took one of her hands between his and ran his fingers thoughtfully over her slender fingers, his eyes coming up to meet hers as he finally murmured, 'What are your dreams, Erin? Tell me about them. Tell me what you want from life.'

She knew that she should be able to respond that her future in London, working in private practice, was what she truly wanted, but now, in all honesty, she couldn't admit to that, only to a vague sense of confusion as she thought about the move she would eventually have to make. 'This moment, you and I here like this— it's all so special to me, Nick. I'm not wishing time away,' she said as she gazed back at him. 'Why do you ask?'

He looked back down at her hand enfolded in his, his eyes hidden from her as he paused thoughtfully, before speaking. Then, with a small sigh escaping his lips as he spoke, he said, 'You know, when I went back to Canada last time, I couldn't stop thinking about you. I wanted to phone you. I must have picked up the phone a dozen times, then replaced it, regretting each time that I didn't dial your number and say what was on my mind.'

'Why didn't you?' Erin stared at him as the soft music flowed around them, her heart suddenly beating very fast.

'You were going to be married.' He shrugged, still not looking at her. 'You had your future with Simon ahead of you, the wedding only two weeks away, and yet . . .' He failed to complete his sentence as he linked his fingers through hers, stroking the smooth skin, bringing up his dark eyes to gaze intently at her. 'Would you have wanted me to?'

It was a question she had often asked herself lately as she'd thought back to those days, and though she knew she had been attracted to Nick she also knew that she had been totally loyal to Simon. The answer had to be in the negative and as she looked down, away from his gaze, it was answer enough.

Nick squeezed her fingers. 'You loved him very much, didn't you?'

Erin felt a fleeting sadness but the memory of Simon was no longer painful, and as she raised her eyes she knew that what she had felt for him was in no way comparable to what she had begun to feel for this man sitting opposite her, his eyes fixed on her face.

'Nick, I—' she began, but was cut short by a sudden sharp noise that seemed at first unfamiliar as she saw Nick's eyes flash and his forehead crease into a frown.

He released her hand and drew back, reaching into his jacket pocket and sliding out his pager. For a moment Erin waited breathlessly, aware that Max was on call over the weekend and that the only reason he would page them would be for an emergency.

Nick looked up from the pager, meeting Erin's eyes. 'It's bad news, Erin. Alec's collapsed. He's been taken to hospital with a massive heart attack. I'm afraid we need to return quickly.'

Without saying more, they rose, Nick explaining the cancellation of their meal to the girl at Reception as they left. Hurrying out to the car, Erin felt a wave of apprehension wash over her as Nick climbed in and started the engine. He cast her a swift smile, but his face was white and taut and Erin could only guess at what might lie ahead of them.

CHAPTER ELEVEN

Max met them as they walked into the ICU, his expression indicating that the situation was grave. The three of them adjourned to the waiting lounge where Alec's son, Gavin, was sitting. He told them briefly that his father's condition was critical and that Rosemary, his mother, was at Alec's bedside. They had been in conversation for only a few moments when a doctor approached and came to stand in front of Gavin, drawing him discreetly to one side.

'Dad didn't make it,' Gavin said shakily after the doctor had left. 'I must go to Mum ... she'll be needing me.'

They offered their murmured condolences to Gavin, but Erin was aware that they were all too shaken to think clearly. 'Is there anything we can do?' she asked helplessly, but Gavin shook his head, clearly very distressed, saying that he would be in touch with them the following day.

Afterwards, as they tried to come to terms with the news of Alec's death, Max thrust his hand through his hair and attempted to explain that Alec had been taken ill while at the dry-dockyard where he had been working on *Agatha*, his boat. Max had arrived at the hospital shortly after the ambulance and Rosemary. He had called Gavin and then it had just been a question of waiting.

'Does Alissa know?' Erin asked, but Max shook his head.

'She's out with the children. I'll have to break it to her when I get home.' He shrugged his shoulders heavily. 'She and Alec have known each other for years. It was Alec who suggested that she and her first husband move to Hayford Minster to form a partnership. She'll be devastated, of course.'

Erin nodded as they walked in silence along the corridor towards the exit, words for the moment failing each one of them.

'He told me recently that he found it difficult to slow down,' Nick said eventually. 'I think that, although he loved his boat and was eager to spend time with his family, in his heart of hearts he found the concept of retirement very daunting.'

Max nodded as he held the door open and they walked through. 'Yes, he was always an active man—I just wish we had known earlier about his heart problems.'

Nick stopped as they walked into the fresh air. 'That's a point we'll never be able to resolve. Alec must have known he stood a chance of genetic heart disease. All I can think is that he handled it in his own way, and I suppose that is what we all would prefer to do as doctors.'

Max shrugged. 'Well, I'd better go home and get this over with. By Monday Gavin will have contacted us and we'll have some idea of when they will hold the funeral.'

Nick and Erin watched Max walk away, his head bowed, and Nick slid an arm around Erin's waist, looking down at her in concern. 'Are you all right?' he asked gently, and she nodded, emotion welling up inside her as they turned, walking slowly back to the car, her legs feeling like jelly, the shock now taking its toll.

*   *   *

Later, when Erin recalled the following days and the funeral, which had been so well attended by all those who had known Alec, she was continually surprised by the depth of feeling in the town.

Alec Rogers had spent most of his professional life working in Hayford Minster. He had established a reputation for kindness and generosity, giving his time and attention to all his patients. Tributes overflowed the small chapel of remembrance in the Minster, and Gavin and Rosemary were touched by such affection.

While Nick and Max coped with surgery, Erin, Alissa and Kirstie represented the practice at the funeral held on the Friday of the following week. During the service Erin thought of how she had come to this place and experienced so many emotions under its ancient roof.

She found herself recalling the day she had waited for Simon in her beautiful wedding gown, unable to believe that he wasn't coming, her father's hand going over hers as she'd tried to absorb the awful truth. Then there had been the peaceful evening a few months later when she had sat in the quiet of the church, alone, struggling to accept what had happened to her.

And this year she had attended baby Jake's christening as his godmother, standing next to Nick, unaware that Simon had been waiting outside for her this time. As they stood to sing the last hymn, the irony wasn't lost on Erin. She was preparing to leave a place that she had once planned to define as home. And in her heart of hearts she knew that Nick had been right.

She was running away, but not from the ghosts of her time with Simon . . .

She was leaving Hayford Minster because she found herself unable to commit herself to the man she really loved. Scarred by what had happened to her before, she couldn't find it in herself to trust again.

As the Rogers family left the church and Erin joined them with Alissa and Kirstie, her last thoughts were for Alec. He had left behind a legacy of goodwill and fond memories. She felt that was what he would have wanted as an epitaph and that he had lived his life with Rosemary, his practice and his beloved Aggie to its fullest.

Suddenly she wished Nick was walking beside her, his fingers linked into hers as they had so often been over these last few months, and that they were looking ahead to the future, intending to seize it together.

*　　　*　　　*

At the practice meeting following the funeral, the general air was sombre, although Erin felt that everyone was trying to get back to normal and re-establish routine.

It was decided that Kirstie, the practice manager, and Jane, the secretary, would make a concerted effort to find a replacement rather than a locum for the practice. Alissa had agreed to work part time from December and, hopefully, by then there would be further news of an applicant.

Erin realised that the last thing she wanted to do was to make things difficult by leaving the practice understaffed. She offered to stay on until someone was found, but her heart wasn't in it, nor, it seemed, was Nick's. They deliberately avoided the question of her leaving date, and as November engulfed Hayford Minster in seasonal mists Erin realised that their lovemaking was shadowed by an unspoken tension that neither of them acknowledged.

Perhaps it was the time of the year, she reasoned with herself as she lay in Nick's arms

199

in his large double bed, his flat more often than not their intimate retreat. Or perhaps the dismay that had followed Alec's passing had left an unseasonal gloom.

However, there was an upside to the month with the news that Gladys and Tom Knight had been found places together in a good nursing home, which was very welcome. Erin visited them there one Friday in early November. Although Tom's dementia was taking its course, Gladys was being aided by the understanding staff and recovering from her hip operation.

'I'm just relieved I'm able to be with him,' Gladys told her as they sat together in the residents' lounge while Tom napped. 'I don't know if we'll ever go home, but I'm putting that right out of my head. Just living each day as it comes,' she said resignedly.

It was a remark that was echoed by Pauline Ford who attended Erin's surgery the following Monday for a checkup. Erin examined her and was relieved to find that, although she was still very thin, she was well and healthy and the bruising had now disappeared. Dressed in her former smart fashion and neatly bobbed hairstyle, Erin took this as a positive sign as her patient sat quietly in the chair by her desk.

'Des and I are going to try to make a go of it,' she explained. 'Mark and I are finished—I know it would have ended up badly, but I just seemed to be unable to do anything about it. Whether it was love or not . . .' Her voice tailed off as she looked wistfully at Erin. 'I've also given up my job. Des says he'll come home more often and we're going to try to spend some time as a family, something we had lost sight of with the pressure of our careers before we separated.'

'I'm pleased for you both,' Erin said with genuine relief. 'I'm sure things will work out,' she added as Pauline rose to her feet.

'I hope so, Dr Brooks.'

Erin said goodbye, hoping that the effort both the Fords were putting into their marriage would pay dividends. Certainly their daughter would now have both her parents under one roof and, hopefully, with perseverance they would achieve results.

Her eyes dropped to the letter on her desk and she leaned forward to read it again. It was from the consultant at the hospital who had seen Esme Kelly. The mammogram and fine-needle aspirate cytology showed no suspicious features, giving Esme a clean bill of health. It seemed, Erin thought as she made a note to ask Esme to come in to see her, that despite the personal sadness that November had brought with it at least two of her patients would end the year on a happier note.

Fergus completed the portrait and Nick collected it a few days after the funeral. There seemed little point in presenting it until Christmas. The timing would be more appropriate, Nick suggested, and Erin agreed.

One Sunday evening in the middle of November they found themselves sitting at a supper table prepared for two in Nick's flat, the candlelight flickering around the room. The portrait of the Darvills hung on the facing wall, a temporary home before Christmas where Fergus's work could be viewed in quiet contemplation.

Erin had served a traditional roast—chicken, crunchy potatoes and fresh vegetables. Last month's unhappy event was now past and Nick reached out to take her hand, his thoughts, though, seeming to be elsewhere.

'It was a delicious meal,' he murmured distractedly, as though he'd been about to say something else but had changed his mind. He added, 'Did you manage to find your way around the kitchen?'

Since the kitchen of both her flat and Nick's were identical, the cooking of the meal had posed her no problems and she shrugged, feeling that there was something she didn't quite understand about the mood of the evening and that the conversation was stalling for some reason. 'I didn't have too much trouble . . .' she said, hearing the tightness of her own voice and wondering if Nick wasn't relaxed because of being on call.

His brown eyes glimmered in the

candlelight, his hair thrust back over his head revealing strong features and grainy male skin as he toyed with a fork that lay beside his plate. He had become so familiar to her; she felt she knew every inch of him as she had run her fingers over his body with her eyes closed and had savoured the moments as they'd lain in bed, his long, muscled form curled around her at night.

'Do you think they'll like it?' he said after a while as he glanced up at the portrait, his tone hesitant.

She nodded. 'It's a perfect likeness—Aaron's smile, Sasha's dark eyes, Alissa's expression and Bas's cheekiness. Max, with Jake in his arms . . . Everything is there. Fergus has captured the real feeling of family.'

'I think so, too.' He added pensively, 'The perfect family . . .'

Erin bit her lip as she swallowed. Was he thinking of what he could have achieved with Sherry? Was he regretting his decision to return to England? Was there still a possibility that their relationship would be rekindled when she visited? Was that why he was so distant this evening?

'Jane told me today that a Dr Bob Lomax is interested in our advertisement and wants to speak to us with a view to taking up a partnership,' he said suddenly. 'It seems he's not from around this area, but from the north. He recently married and he's looking for a house and a career in a country environment. The initial details sound hopeful.'

Erin felt a chill inside her as she knew that this piece of news heralded her own departure, and that after Christmas she would soon be leaving the place she had come to know and love as home. More than that, she would be leaving Nick, and it seemed that he was in no way attempting to stop her, which only served to confirm her thoughts about Sherry and the place she held in his heart.

'So that brings us to the next question.' He looked at her steadily. 'We need to set up a meeting with him and, if we all agree, arrange a date that ties in with your plans to leave.'

Erin nodded, managing a smile. 'That's good news,' she said in a voice that didn't seem quite steady. 'When do you suggest?'

Nick watched her, his eyes going slowly over her face. 'Some time during the week,' he said quietly, 'since next weekend I have to go up to London.' It was then that she realised that this was the reason he had been preoccupied. She felt an almost physical stab of pain at her ribs as he added expressionlessly, 'Sherry's in England, staying with a friend—'

Just then the phone rang and, giving a small sigh, he rose from the table, his sentence left unfinished as he answered it. Erin sat there as his voice drifted around the room, her thoughts and emotions in chaos. Somehow she had known deep inside that Nick's affair with Sherry was not ended. As she glanced at the tall figure standing by the bureau, his head tilted against the receiver as he scribbled an address on the notepad, dismay and desperation washed over her.

She had fallen in love against her better judgement, all logical reasoning seeming to have deserted her, and, worse, she hadn't learned by her experience with Simon, allowing her heart to rule her head once more.

With eyes misting, she rose, clearing the table in order to cover her distress, eager for Nick to be gone on the call so that she could give way to the tears that burned at the back of her eyes.

*   *   *

Alissa glanced at her watch and wondered if Kirsten had found the strained apple she had left on the top shelf of the fridge. Resisting the urge to phone home, she smiled to herself, realising that Kirsten, now a two-week veteran of supervising Jake, was entirely capable of feeding him lunch!

It had been a surprisingly easy transition, returning to work, in a strange way made more natural by Alec's death. Alissa felt a pang of sadness when she thought of her old friend, but knew that he would have been the first to say that life had to go on.

Brief thoughts of their friendship passed

through her mind, then with an effort of will she turned her thoughts to the present and to the meeting with Bob Lomax.

They had all gathered for supper last night at the house. She had prepared a small buffet and they'd talked as they'd eaten, making the event a social occasion and therefore more relaxed. Felicity Lomax, Bob's wife, proved to be a bright, pleasant young woman who had applied for a teaching post at the local comprehensive. Bob seemed a likeable man and Alissa was sure that he was right for the partnership. Even so, this interview at lunchtime would resolve any professional doubts one way or another.

Her thoughts drifted to Nick and Erin. They had seemed distant last night and Erin had looked pale and distracted. Nick wouldn't be present at the meeting today, though he had given his full approval of Bob Lomax.

It wasn't like Nick to take unplanned time off and Alissa's forehead was pleated in a thoughtful frown as Erin walked into her room. 'All ready?' she asked, and smiled, though Alissa's suspicions were reinforced as she studied her friend's pale and unusually tense face.

'Has Bob arrived?' Alissa enquired as she rose to her feet and gathered her bag.

'Yes, we've made coffee in the staffroom and the girls on Reception are taking appointments for two-thirty onwards so we have an hour at least for the interview.'

Erin avoided her gaze, chewing on her bottom lip. Alissa knew then that there was something wrong. She had hoped that the relationship between Nick and Erin would have deepened and that Erin would have changed her mind about leaving, for not only would two female doctors have been of great benefit to the practice but Erin was a good friend and godmother to Jake.

'How long will Nick be away?' Alissa asked as they walked to the door, wondering if it was Nick's absence that was causing the problem.

'He's taking Monday off,' Erin responded tonelessly, 'so it will be four days in all.' Pausing before she opened the door, she finally let out a small sigh and met Alissa's gaze for the first time. 'Alissa, has Nick said anything to you about Sherry Tate?'

Alissa shook her head. 'No, nothing at all. She phoned to ask for his number and I gave it. I know there was some suggestion that she might be visiting . . . Is she in England?'

Erin's green eyes were confused as she nodded. 'Yes. Nick is meeting her in London.'

Alissa looked astonished. 'I had no idea. He certainly didn't mention it to me and I'm sure Max would have said if he knew. I did wonder why Nick was taking time off . . . Are you sure it's because of Sherry?'

Erin nodded slowly. 'He told me himself.'

'But their relationship is over,' Alissa

207

protested after a few moments' thought. 'Surely Nick has explained that?'

'He rarely mentions her,' Erin said quietly, clenching her hands together and glancing at Alissa with a deep frown. 'If, as you believe, their relationship is over, why would he meet her?'

'There must be some explanation,' Alissa responded. Erin looked up at her and shrugged.

'I'm afraid we've avoided the subject this week and, in view of me leaving in the New Year . . .' Erin's voice shook and she failed to complete her sentence.

'Erin,' Alissa said, her expression softening as she witnessed her friend's consternation, 'it's clear Nick is very fond of you. He wouldn't hurt you, I'm certain of that.'

'Not intentionally,' Erin agreed quietly, 'but after Simon it's not easy to trust again. Besides which, what can the future hold when our lives lie in different directions?'

'Do you love him?' Alissa asked gently, and after a few moments Erin sighed, then nodded silently, her anxious eyes revealing the truth.

'In that case,' Alissa remarked softly, 'the best made plans can be changed. Trust your feelings for Nick and his for you. Don't let this opportunity pass you by, Erin.'

Just then a knock came on the door and Erin opened it fully, revealing the tall figure of Jane, who peered in at them with a curious frown. 'Is everything all right?' she said, looking from one to the other. 'There aren't any problems . . .?'

'No, none, thank you, Jane. We're on our way now.' Alissa glanced at Erin who smiled at her briefly, before walking into the corridor.

As they made their way to the interview Alissa reflected on all she had just learned, yet despite her words of reassurance she felt just as dismayed as Erin that Nick was seeing Sherry again.

*   *   *

Despite being on call over the weekend, four days seemed like an eternity and it wasn't until Tuesday morning at the surgery that Erin saw Nick again. They were both due to start early surgeries and she was hurrying towards the office when he caught her arm roughly and, drawing her to one side in the hallway, muttered, 'Have you a few moments before you start?'

She hadn't heard him coming up behind her, and almost before she nodded her agreement he was pulling her into his room, thrusting the door closed with his foot. Leaning her against it, his mouth came down over hers in a demanding kiss, seeking entry to her mouth with an urgency that overwhelmed her.

In that moment everything else was

forgotten. Her arms went around his neck, his tongue demanding her response with a passion that left her breathless, and as he breathed heavily against her she felt the familiar ache of her need, responding to his.

'Oh, my darling, I've missed you,' he whispered huskily, his arms restraining her movement as he captured her against the door. 'I wanted to come up to you last night, but there was no sign of anyone . . .'

'I was on call,' she breathed shakily. 'I saw your car when I came back from a visit—it must have been almost midnight . . .'

He nodded. 'I didn't want to disturb you.'

She wished he had and had put her out of her misery, her doubts tormenting her every second of the day and night. Seeing no lights on in his flat, she had let herself into her own, aching to be with him, to talk to him, to ask him the many questions that had kept her in anguish. By this morning she felt she had exhausted all the possibilities of her tireless imagination.

'Did you miss me?' he groaned, his voice low and sexy, and she could only nod, kissing him back, wanting him now more than ever. He had assured her he had missed her with his first words, and his embrace was urgent and demanding. Could she really believe that during the time he'd been away he hadn't succumbed to his old love?

'Listen, why don't we get some food in

tonight?' he breathed against her cheek. 'I'm not on call and neither are you. Oh, Erin, I just want to hold you . . . to be alone with you . . .'

'Me, too,' she whispered, careless now of what had happened in the four days they had been apart and needing only the reassurance he could give her. They had so little time left. Did it really matter what had happened in London as long as he was here now, telling her he'd missed her and that all that mattered was each other?

The part of her brain that had so conveniently blanked off that which was distasteful to her was winning, and she gave herself up to one more deep kiss, his words of promise lingering softly in the air as they held each other.

He had returned and still wanted her. And, for the moment, that was enough.

*　　　*　　　*

That evening, the urgency of their desire overcame all need to eat, and the take-away meal they had bought remained uneaten along with a still-corked bottle of red wine. In Nick's big double bed they clung together. Their kisses were filled with a passion that elated and shocked her, for nothing ever before had come close to this.

There seemed a new dimension between them, a fierce need that didn't allow them words or stolen whispers but an almost animal-like urgency to make love and fulfil each other's need. They lay afterwards, exhausted and entwined in one another's arms, the sleep that overcame them washing through their limbs with a drug-like quality as the hours of the evening closed in around them.

Erin woke as the Minster clock struck one, wondering for a moment where she was. Sensing her wakefulness, Nick turned towards her and kissed her, bringing his hands over her breasts that were aching for his touch. He, too, was ready to make love, and in the early hours of the morning they found a new rhythm, slower and more sensual, lingering over their feast as if they were discovering each other once more.

Perhaps their fulfilment overwhelmed the need for explanations. That was what Erin decided, hours later, when they sat at breakfast and Nick mentioned his trip to London for the first time. He spoke of Sherry in a detached way, as though he had spent only a short time in her company, drinking coffee at one of the stores.

The rest of the weekend, he said, he had been spent with a friend with whom he had made contact while Christmas shopping, and touring the City had filled the remaining hours.

'I missed you, my darling,' he assured her once more, his eyes burning into her as he

212

leaned across the breakfast table and kissed her full mouth. She wanted to believe him. And why shouldn't she?

But deep inside her she feared he wasn't telling her the truth. Feeling his hands on her arms, drawing her up and against him, his mouth pressing urgently over hers, she ignored the little voice inside that warned her she might never know it.

CHAPTER TWELVE

Erin removed the last shining red bell attached to the Christmas tree in the waiting room, trying not to think the same thought as she had on so many occasions over the last week. It was the last time she would ever do this, her small Christmas ritual—packing away the decorations, stripping the tree bare and returning the box in which the decorations were kept to the storeroom.

'Did you have a good Christmas and New Year, Dr Brooks?' someone said, jolting her out of her thoughts. She turned to see Mathew Sibson, holding what looked like a bottle of wine wrapped in green tissue paper.

'Oh . . . yes, fine, thanks, Mathew.' She glanced at the open door of the surgery as the first patients of the cold January day made their way into the waiting room. 'What about you?'

'As you can see, the ankle's mended.' He grinned. 'And I've stayed out of trouble since then. Er . . . this is for you.' Erin accepted the wine, raising her eyebrows in surprise. 'For me?'

'Hope you like a good red.'

'Yes, as a matter of fact, I do.' She smiled. 'Thank you, Mathew. How are things with you and Gemma?'

'We've split up,' he said, and his smile faded. 'I broke off our engagement and left her father's business. Gemma took it badly but there was nothing I could do. We would have been very unhappy together.'

'I'm sorry to hear that.' Erin paused as she looked at him and saw that he didn't appear to be too upset. 'But, as you say, marriage was obviously not meant to be. Do I take it you're intending to race again?'

He nodded. 'There's a big rally coming up at Easter. I suppose you're also going to tell me I need my brains tested?'

Erin shook her head. 'It's not up to me to do that. Racing seems to be the love of your life.'

'Well, I know one thing now,' he acknowledged readily. 'That it isn't very compatible with relationships. I'll have to get it out of my system before I think of settling down again.'

But Alissa was doubtful that he would ever

214

tire of his addiction to fast cars and speed. At least he hadn't taken the fateful step of marrying Gemma, knowing the way she felt about racing.

Erin watched him walk away, acknowledging that in her own case she could almost feel grateful to Simon now. She would have been trapped in an unhappy marriage with a man who didn't love her or she him had he turned up on their wedding day. This didn't change the circumstances of the manner in which he had let her down, though, but even that now was an event that held no heartache for her. One day, perhaps Mathew Sibson's ex-fiancée would also be able to look back on her broken engagement without regret.

As Erin removed the box of decorations to the cupboard and then went to her own room, she reflected that Christmas had come and gone so swiftly that it seemed impossible that only a week ago the New Year had arrived. She'd lain in Nick's arms as the Minster clock had struck twelve, their private and intimate celebration heralding the newest of January mornings.

Bob Lomax had already begun to carve his niche in the practice, his energy and enthusiasm almost contagious as, despite the cold weather and fresh wave of flu cases, he had applied himself to the long and often fraught surgeries just before the holiday. The fact that he had been forced to spend Boxing

Day in bed with a raging fever hadn't daunted his spirit, and as New Year's Eve had arrived he had recovered in time to take the on-call duty that would have been allotted to her had he still been ill.

As Erin placed Mathew Sibson's bottle aside and resumed her seat at her desk, she heard voices in the corridor—Alissa's light laughter and Bob's pleasant voice which was now familiar to everyone. But as Erin listened to them pass her door, it was Nick who filled her thoughts and the almost unbelievable fact that she would take her last surgery on Friday afternoon. At the weekend she would leave for London and all this—all that she had loved and striven towards—would be part and parcel of the past.

*   *   *

Alissa stared admiringly at the beautiful portrait of her family hanging on the wall that faced the door in the drawing room, a centrepiece which had brought tears to her eyes when Nick and Erin had presented it to them on Christmas Eve.

'But how . . .? When . . .?' She had gasped, then she had understood, recalling the photographs Nick had taken and his mysterious reference to a future gift.

'Better late than never,' Nick had said rather gruffly, as emotion had seized them all when the picture had been held up by Max, and the children had come in to admire their likenesses. Alissa had sensed how close Erin and Nick had been at Christmas and she'd felt sad that they were parting, but Erin had told her that her plans had been made and she would keep to them. Had Nick asked Erin to stay, would the story have ended differently? Alissa wondered now.

Alissa sighed deeply. It seemed there was nothing she could do to prevent two of her closest friends from parting for ever, an unhappy thought with which to start a brand-new year.

*   *   *

'What would you like to do on Friday evening?'

Erin looked up from her study of one of Nick's large black photograph albums, his voice interrupting her thoughts. There were no photographs of Sherry in this book, just beautiful landscapes of Vancouver, Montreal and Winnipeg, places she would have loved to have visited with him. But she quickly brought her mind to the present, closing the album and returning it to the shelf with its companions.

'You'll be on call?' she said as she moved across the room. He held out his arms, his face bearing an expression that seemed to melt her.

'Yes,' he said as she joined him, linking her

arms around his waist, 'but I've been thinking about asking Bob to swap with me—'

'No, don't do that. It doesn't seem fair.' She laid her head against his chest as he drew her against him, running his fingers through her hair and over the soft blue sweater that she wore. 'He was just about on his feet again at New Year, and if he hadn't been fit then we wouldn't have been able to celebrate it with each other.'

'Yes, I suppose you're right,' he murmured above her, the deep rumble of his voice echoing into her ear as she closed her eyes, thinking how she could happily remain for hours in the warm circle of his arms.

She was relieved he couldn't read her mind because at the moment she felt that one of them being on duty on Friday gave some sense of normality to what seemed like a crazy week. Everything seemed tinged with sadness and nostalgia, even the small party the girls at work had thrown in the staffroom. She had forced herself to join in, laughing and talking, ignoring the sense of deep dismay that had settled like an iron weight in the pit of her stomach.

Suddenly Nick gripped her arms and held her gently away from him, looking squarely into her eyes. 'It doesn't have to be our last evening, you know,' he said huskily, and all at once her heart leapt with hope. Was he about to ask her to stay? Was he going to tell her that

218

Sherry was no longer a part of his life? Were the three words that she so desperately wanted to hear, and that he had never said, about to be spoken?

Hope quickly faded as he murmured, 'I can take a weekend off next month. I could drive up to London . . .'

She fought to keep her composure at the half-hearted suggestion, the uncomfortable look in his dark eyes and the instinct inside her that warned he was trying his hardest not to hurt her but to end their relationship as painlessly as possible. 'Yes, perhaps.' She nodded, but she knew that this was the end, this was goodbye.

'We'll have a quiet meal at home, then, and hope that we don't get too many calls. We may be lucky.' His eyes met hers once more, but this time they had recovered from the moment of indecision, his tone lighter, indicating that he, too, wished to say as little as possible on the matter.

They didn't make love that night, just held each other close, neither of them ready for sleep, and she lay in his arms, memorising the patterns the streetlight outside made on the walls of the bedroom. Outside the world went on without change—the neighbour who arrived home in the early hours from his shift work, the milkman who delivered at three a.m. Even the cat that refused to be silenced and sat on the roof of her car, mewing territorially.

She would never forget all this. Simple pleasures. The most tender moments of her existence. These were her albums, her mental gallery of pictures. Nick's warm, strong arms encircling her, his steady breathing and the sound of their hearts, pounding as one.

She would recall them all . . . each last detail . . . and hoard them for a lifetime.

*   *   *

'Erin? It's Bob.' Bob Lomax's voice was faint as the mobile crackled.

'I can just about hear you, Bob. You'll have to speak up.' Erin frowned as the static rattled in her ear.

'I'm outside of one of our patient's houses. A Tina Wyatt. Her husband phoned in late this evening while I was at surgery and I said I'd make a visit. But she's really Nick's patient. She's eight months pregnant and I'm not happy about her. The problem is . . .' The static interrupted again and Bob's voice faded. 'I've come out to the car,' Erin heard next, 'to find the battery completely dead. The daft thing was, I left my lights on. A kid from next door knocked to let me know . . .'

Erin felt sympathetic as she recalled how she had done exactly the same thing early one summer's morning and Nick had helped her. Since that time she had taken the precaution of keeping a spare battery in the garage. 'How can I help, Bob?' she almost shouted into the phone.

'Don't worry about me . . . phone for the services . . .' The reply was distorted. Just thought I'd let Nick know . . . getting Mrs Wyatt into hospital straight away . . . possible Caesar.'

'I'll get a message to him,' Erin offered at once. 'Our cars are the same model, aren't they? I've a spare battery in the garage—I'll bring it for you. What's the address?'

Bob was reluctant to accept her offer but finally she persuaded him to allow her to help. Erin scribbled down the address, recalling the rather isolated area just outside of the town.

'There's ice on the road . . . be careful . . . especially on . . .' The static overwhelmed the line and Erin grimaced. She paused for a few seconds more, then decided there was no point in listening any longer. Paging Nick with a message about Tina Wyatt, she then threw on her coat and grabbed her case.

Hurrying out to the line of garages that were situated behind the rows of terraced houses, she almost slipped on black ice. The frost had hardened into a thin sheet over the pavements, a fact she should have taken more heed of as she unlocked and lifted the up-and-over door.

Minutes later she was driving into the darkness, and as the town lights faded behind her thick woodland engulfed the long, lonely road ahead. Suddenly a fox ran into the road and hesitated. Its beautiful ginger coat shone against the white frost. The creature paused, transfixed by the powerful lights of her car.

Erin braked.

The fox leapt to safety but a split second later a luminous danger sign sent danger signals into her brain. Something Bob had said . . .

In slow motion, it seemed, the skid she was entering formed a life of its own. The ghostly trees, the steep bank that was fenced with boundary wire . . . In one horrifying tangle of erratic light they merged together as she felt the car go out of control.

Then there was the sensation of being weightless as she grappled with a useless steering-wheel. The car ricocheted against something and lifted into the air. Finally, and most hauntingly, an eerie silence encompassed her as the seconds turned into an eternity and everything went black.

*   *   *

The sound of a car's hooter was the first noise to penetrate her dark world, and even then it was as though it was coming from miles away. When it stopped abruptly, she felt rather than saw someone's presence as she was gently lifted away from the steering-wheel. Familiar fingers linked into hers, pressing them gently as she tried in vain to return their grip.

'It's all right, Erin, you're going to be all right. I'm with you all the way, every step, I'm here.'

Was she dreaming? Was it Nick? In the darkness that seemed to grip her mind and paralyse her thoughts, she knew it was him. She knew that something terrible had happened to her, but he was there— somewhere—and she clung to this thought.

As they cut her free from the wreck, the lights around her and the noise of the rescue team slowly became a painful reality. It was Nick who administered the injection to ease her pain, fitted the collar tenderly around her neck and attended to the drip, before allowing them to remove her to the ambulance.

He was there, holding her hand, constantly reassuring her. He whispered he would always be with her, that he would never let her go. And that he loved her.

He loved her . . .

In her twilight world she heard those words and knew that, whatever happened, her soul was reaching out to him and calling back that she loved him, too.

CHAPTER THIRTEEN

'Don't say a word. Just open it.'

'But—'

'Look, I'll help you . . .'

Nick stood beside the hospital bed, looking wonderful, Erin thought, in dark blue jeans and a crisp navy shirt. His eyes met hers for a moment as he eased the large square parcel he had brought her onto the coverlet of the bed, carefully avoiding the plaster cast around her leg.

Because of this and the tenderness of her fractured ribs it wasn't easy to assist him but, attempting to remove the silvery wrapping paper, Erin managed to restrain her excitement as Nick's long fingers slipped the silver bow and peeled back the paper.

For a moment her breath caught in her throat as she stared at the gilt frame and the painting encompassed within it. 'It's *me*?' she breathed incredulously.

He laughed softly as he sat down. 'Of course it's you.'

She stared at the uncanny likeness of herself, a pair of sea-green eyes meeting hers with a studied calm, the full lips below turned up into a soft smile. 'Nick, it's beautiful,' she said at last. 'It's so lovely . . .'

'*You* are lovely,' he told her as his eyes went

slowly over her. 'Haven't I told you so often enough over the past two weeks?'

Erin tore her eyes away from the picture and met his gaze. Since her accident a fortnight ago he had been constantly by her side, visiting the hospital whenever he had a spare hour, phoning her, sending flowers, willing her recovery. As for herself, she couldn't yet quite believe that so much had happened on that fateful, freezing night, events which had caused her future to be changed at a stroke.

Her move to London was now out of the question, another candidate accepted in her place. Her job in private practice was but a distant memory—one that had obviously meant little to her since she had not wasted a moment's regret on its passing.

As for the crash, she remembered snatches of the car turning a somersault on that icy bend. Miraculously, it had seemed, Nick had been the first on the scene, the message she had conveyed to him by means of the pager bringing him swiftly from his last house call to follow her within minutes along the same stretch of road.

Recognising the colour and shape of her car, he had fought his way through the tangle of metal to reach her and had whispered those words of comfort she had heard in her semi-conscious world.

It had been no trick of her imagination that

he had been with her throughout the journey to hospital and had remained with her until many hours later he'd finally left Intensive Care, reassured by the doctors that she would pull through.

Time had passed slowly since that night. The broken ribs which had so dangerously threatened to pierce her lung in the first few days were now beginning to heal, though her fractured tibia would take longer to mend. But she had adjusted herself to this now and was prepared for the six months' wait that would be needed for the bones in her leg to sustain a full recovery.

She had been very lucky—was lucky to be alive—and she knew it. As she gazed at the portrait she felt tears spring to her eyes, emotion suddenly overwhelming her as she bit down hard on her lip, trying to compose herself.

'The portrait was meant to be a going-away present,' Nick said quietly, leaning his elbows on the bed, staring at the smiling image of the dark-haired girl with incredible green eyes. 'I hoped that each time you looked at it, you'd remember me.'

Erin swallowed, completely overwhelmed. Despite every effort at control, she knew she was fighting a losing battle with her emotions, and as he took the picture from her and lowered it to the floor one small tear escaped from the comer of her eye and fell onto the sleeve of her dressing gown. 'Oh, Nick,' she fumbled, 'how could I ever forget what we shared?'

'In time you would have.' He looked at her, his eyes reflecting the anguish he'd concealed. 'Wouldn't you?'

She could hardly trust herself to speak as she shook her head. 'No, I would never have forgotten. You must know that.'

His voice was husky as he raised his hand to her cheek, tenderly smoothing away the dampness that glistened there. 'You thought that I was still involved with Sherry, didn't you? You really did imagine I was in love with another woman when you were in my arms, when we were making love—when all I wanted was for us to be together.' His voice was incredulous. 'Well, thank God I've had some time to do a little research since your accident. I see now why you were so hell-bent on leaving me. It was Alissa who finally told me that you had somehow decided that my time away just before Christmas was spent with Sherry—and that nothing that she had been able to say had convinced you that Sherry was no longer a part of my life.'

Painfully aware that the thin coat of foundation she had managed to apply before visiting time couldn't hide her embarrassment, Erin stared down at her clasped hands. 'I . . . I didn't know what to believe,' she murmured, unable to look at him. 'I knew Sherry had phoned you several times and I assumed that you wanted to see her again. I came to the conclusion that, despite what we shared together, she was still in your heart.'

One eyebrow lifted as he mocked her gently with his eyes. 'Oh, Erin, it was nothing like that, although, looking back, I can see that it would have been easy to make such an interpretation. But the truth was that Sherry suggested she visit me and stay in Hayford Minster. That, of course, was the last thing I wanted. I had no intention of allowing the little time I had left with you to be spoilt by unwelcome reminders of the past. My plan was to head her off—that's all I could think of.'

'You mean, you didn't spend the weekend with her?' Erin said weakly.

'Erin, I barely spent an hour with her. We found there was nothing we had to say to one another, and the meeting was a complete waste of time.'

'But—but you were away for so long,' Erin said helplessly. 'I couldn't help but think . . .'

'Well, that was where the masterplan backfired,' he broke in with a deep sigh. 'I spent a day dawdling around the City, unable to concentrate on anything and wishing away the time, then I drove back to the New Forest and stopped at Fergus's studio. God knows, I was miserable enough when I asked him to paint this portrait from a photograph I had with me. Over a few jugs of his home brew I poured out my woeful story—that the lady I was so desperately in love with was intent on leaving me. He suggested I give you some space and that seemed a reasonable enough idea at the time.'

'You stayed with *Fergus* that weekend?' Erin said in amazement.

'I hoped you'd miss me so much you'd throw yourself into my arms on my return and swear we'd never be apart again. It was crazy, I know. But, then, I was a desperate man, clutching at straws.'

'But if only I'd known, Nick. Why didn't you tell me?'

'You seemed so focused, so sure of what you wanted.' He looked at her calmly. 'Remember, Simon was as much a part of your life once as Sherry was of mine. So I decided to wait, give you time and pray that I'd still be in there with a chance if our relationship deepened. The problem was that I discovered I'd left it too late, that you were determined to leave Hayford Minster for a bright new future in private practice and that there was nothing I could do or say to stop it.'

'I was running away, I know that now.' Erin met his gaze and nodded. 'You were right, Nick, but I just couldn't accept it at the time.'

'Even so, I shouldn't have said that . . .'

She smiled, slowly shaking her head. 'You made me realise that I was blaming Simon for everything, refusing to admit my part in the failure of our relationship.'

He was silent for a moment as he gazed at her then, leaning forward, he raised her hand and brushed his lips across her knuckles. 'I could have lost you,' he muttered grimly, 'and I almost did.'

Erin lowered her eyes in shame for she had her own guilt, recalling how jealousy had tortured her all those months. 'I saw those photographs of Sherry in your albums,' she acknowledged regretfully. 'I was so convinced she was still a part of your life . . . she's so beautiful. I couldn't believe you didn't want her still.'

'Erin, don't you realise that I haven't been able to get you out of my thoughts since we first met?' he said incredulously. 'I was convinced you were returning to London in order to be near Simon. I wanted to tell you I loved you, was about to so many times, but I couldn't have handled a rejection—or your pity—so I kept quiet, hoping against hope that you'd change your mind about the job.'

She shook her head slowly. 'You would have had neither a rejection nor my pity, Nick. I've loved you—I've always loved you. I know now that I was never in love with Simon—a fact I was unwilling to admit until I discovered what loving someone was really was about.'

'And what is it that you want now, Erin?' His dark eyes searched her face, seeming to bore deeply into her mind as he gazed intently at her. 'I asked you once before what your dreams were and you said you were content to live for the present. Has that changed in any way?'

'You must know that it has.' She yearned to be held and let out a soft, frustrated sigh as she tried to move, giving a little yelp as she moved too swiftly.

He was instantly by her side, resting one strong thigh carefully on the side of her bed, clasping her gently in his arms. 'I'm afraid to touch you, darling,' he whispered huskily, 'but, I promise you, I'm going to make up for lost time when you're better.'

Her heart began to pound as she gazed up at him. 'Oh, Nick, we really *do* have a future together?'

'A lifetime,' he replied without hesitation, tipping up her chin to look squarely into her eyes. 'It took the accident to make me realise I would never let you go again, no matter what happened.' He frowned slightly as he added softly, 'Do you remember our first kiss the year before last—that brief farewell kiss?'

'Yes, I remember . . . after our trip out to Briar House, just before you left England . . .'

'Well, one day we're going back there and setting the record straight. I'm going to kiss you again and tell you how much I love you, and in years to come we'll tell our children the story of how our romance began in the heart of a fairy-tale forest. Then, when all the talking is over . . .' And before she could reply his mouth came down on hers, the words he murmured against her lips an exquisite promise that was to seal their dreams for ever.